I0578669

THE SOUL BOND

RITE WORLD: BLACKTHORN HUNTERS
ACADEMY BOOK 3

JULIANA HAYGERT

COPYRIGHT

This book is a work of fiction. Names, characters, places, and incidents either are products of the author's imagination or are used fictitiously. Any resemblance to actual persons, living or dead, events, or locales is entirely coincidental.

Copyright © 2020 by Juliana Haygert

All rights reserved. This book or any portion thereof may not be reproduced or used in any manner whatsoever without the express written permission of the publisher except for the use of brief quotations in a book review.

Manufactured in the United States of America.

First Edition September 2019

www.JulianaHaygert.com

Edited by H. Danielle Crabtree

Cover design by Covers by Juan

Any trademark, service marks, product names, or names featured are the property of their respective owners, and are used only for reference. There is no implied endorsement if one of these terms is used.

✣ Created with Vellum

AUTHOR'S NOTE

I HOPE you enjoy reading *The Soul Bond*!

DON'T FORGET to sign up for my Newsletter to find out about new releases, cover reveals, giveaways, and more!

If you want to see exclusive teasers, help me decide on covers, read excerpts, talk about books, etc, join my reader group on Facebook: Juliana's Club!

RITE WORLD

Welcome to the RITE WORLD!

Rite World:
The Vampire Heir (Book 1)
The Witch Queen (Book 2)
The Immortal Vow (Book 3)
The Warlock Lord (Book 4)
The Wolf Consort (Book 5)
The Crystal Rose (Book 6)
The Wolf Forsaken (Book 7)
The Fae Bound (Book 8)
The Blood Pact (Book 9)

Rite World: Blackthorn Hunters Academy
The Demons Kiss (Book 1)
The Hunter Secret (Book 2)
The Soul Bond (Book 3)
The Shadow Trials (Book 4)
The Immortal Vow (Book 5)

MAP

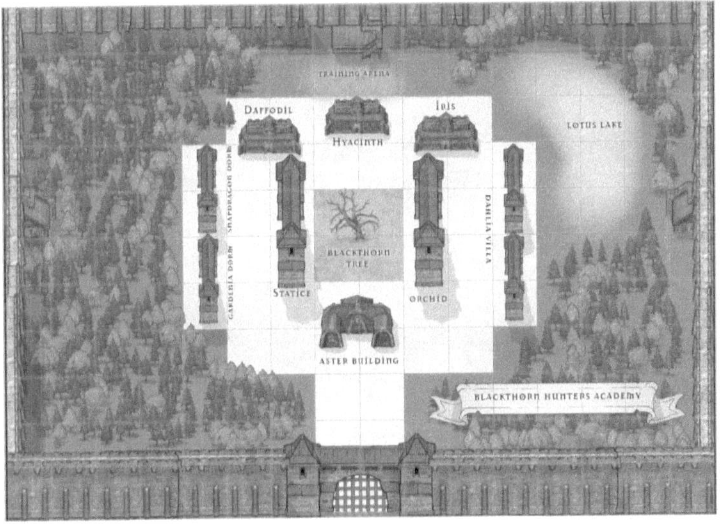

Map of Blackthorn Hunters Academy

Click here to view the map in a separate browser.

1

ERIN

"ARE YOU READY?" Claire asked.

I glanced around the small, loft apartment. We had lived in here for a few months during the summer break, but I had grown attached to it. Though the apartment was located on a quiet side of Chasseur Ville, Claire and I had been mostly isolated from the rest of the town. In our loft, there were no classes, no training, no bitchy girls, or cocky guys. There were no demons, no secrets, no battles to be fought.

It had been simple, relaxing, unmemorable.

During the past year of my life, everything had been big, crazy, and surprising. Whenever I could have freaking unmemorable, I would take it.

"Do we need to go back?" I whispered, wishing we could pretend to be normal girls for a bit longer.

So much had happened last semester—I had joined a half-demon army, found out a bit more about the Demon Kissed Queens' legend, fought a crazy demon set on killing me, discovered I had a half-brother, and fallen in love with the man who was supposed to be my soulmate, but who rejected me time and time again. It made me wonder what would happen with this semester. Because I was a freaking demonic princess, daughter of Brikan, the king of the underworld, nothing would ever be simple, relaxing, and unmemorable for me.

Claire put her arm around my shoulders. "We do," she said with a smile. Her blond curls were growing, but she didn't like them when they bounced in her face, so she kept tying a few strands back. "I wish we could stay holed up here too, but we can't."

Like me, Claire had suffered a painful heartbreak. She had fallen for Tanner, my half-brother, while he had been possessed by a demon. He had been horrible to her.

"It's important that we go back to the academy," she added.

Was it, though?

But I knew it was important. I wasn't safe anywhere else, not even here in Chasseur Ville, because of whose daughter I was. Even though this place was filled with demon hunters, all of them had either never exercised the occupation or were retired. If King Brikan invaded the village with his princes and legions of higher demons, everyone in Chasseur Ville would die because of me.

At the academy, the students were training to be demon hunters, plus the full-fledged demon hunters were a snap of the fingers away, and moreover, the headmaster was there. Randall had become the first demon hunter many eons ago. He was the founder and headmaster of the Blackthorn Hunters Academy, super powerful with magic that no one else had, and immortal. So far, I had seen him kill a prince of the underworld and a higher demon as if they were bugs under his shoe.

If I wanted to stand a chance against my father, I needed the protection of the academy.

I could see the reason in that, but it didn't make me want to go back any more.

I let out a sigh. "All right. Let's go."

I picked up my duffel bag from the floor and headed out of the loft with Claire. The rest of our things were already inside her car—a small sedan she had gotten as a late birthday gift from her grandmother last year. It was a good thing too. Otherwise, I would have to call my mother to come pick us up, which I seriously didn't want to do. Although my mother had defended me to the school council when they wanted to kick me out after finding out about my father—they had wanted to kill me, actually—we were still not on good terms. She had offered to let me to stay at her townhouse with her at Dahlia Villa inside the academy, like we had done during winter break, but this time, I couldn't. So she rented this apartment for me. I ended up convincing Claire to ask her father to let her join me, and surprisingly, he agreed. Which didn't make sense because her father, Professor Crimson, had been one of the most vocal against me remaining at the academy last semester.

But I was glad he did, because then I didn't have to spend the last two months alone in here.

After pushing my bag onto the backseat, I sat beside Claire in the front. She glanced one more time to the loft upstairs before turning the engine on and driving away.

I looked out the window, always amazed by the quaint village. It was early Sunday morning and tourists—aka, humans—had probably spent the night doing one of the fun treasure hunts until the middle of the night. The village was quiet. The shops' owners were probably cleaning and stocking up for more games that night.

While staying at the loft, Claire and I avoided going out much, since news about my heritage had spread and some of the demon hunters in town didn't like me, but there was one night in the middle of the summer when we joined the fun: on my twentieth birthday. Claire had convinced me to try the treasure hunt. We lost badly, but we laughed a lot while pursuing the clues and trying to figure out where to look next.

I hadn't felt so carefree and *human* in a long time.

Any happy thoughts I had came crashing down when we passed through the grand academy gates, and Claire parked her car in the underground garage.

We were there.

I was not ready.

More students were arriving at the academy for the semester. Most were dropped off by their parents, but some were allowed to bring their cars.

As they exited their cars and hauled their things to the dorms, they glanced my way as if I were a disease to be eradicated. They whispered among themselves, but I heard certain words. They were talking about me, of course, about how they didn't want me to be here, and how they wished I had been expelled from the academy, or publicly executed.

I hadn't been there for five minutes. This would be one hell of a semester.

"Ignore them," Claire whispered to me as we picked up our bags from the backseat and the trunk. "They don't know what they are talking about."

"Easier said than done," I said through gritted teeth.

On purpose, I was slow to take my bags from the car, and

when I started walking, I took one step every few seconds. By the time I made it to the stairs, most of the students had already marched away.

But a new crop was driving in.

I sighed and started walking normally before anyone caught up with me.

But I skidded to a stop when my mother appeared in front of me. "There you are." She clasped her hands in front of herself. I frowned, not entirely happy to see her. She was so stoic, her gestures so cold, her stare so uncaring ... there was nothing about her that made me like being around her. With her dark hair pulled into a tight ponytail, her fine pressed suit, she looked like a model for neatness and coldness. "I've been calling you. Where's your phone?"

"Turned off inside my bag," I said. We weren't supposed to have our cell phones on while at the academy, and she knew that.

She let out an exasperated sigh. "It doesn't matter now. Come with me."

My frown deepened. "Where to?"

Her hazel eyes flamed. "To my office. I'm not asking, Erin."

I fought the urge to cross my arms. "Are you *not asking* as a professor—" I glanced around to make sure no one would hear us. "—or as a mother?"

"Does it matter?" she asked, as if I was an insolent child.

Without waiting for an answer, she turned around and marched away, her heels clicking on the stone pavement of the paths between the buildings.

I closed my eyes and tipped my head up to the sun, as if its bright, warm rays could bathe me and keep my frustration in check. It was such a nice, not too hot summer day. And it had already been ruined by several things.

"Here." Claire reached for my bags. "I'll take these to your dorm."

I resisted her. "You don't need to." My bags weren't too heavy, but she was already carrying hers.

"It's okay." She took them from me. "Just go before she gets mad."

I snorted. "Doesn't that look like she is already mad to you?"

Claire mouthed "go" as she too turned around and started walking toward the Gardenia building, where the female dorms were located. And I followed my mother to the Aster building, which housed the administrative side of the academy.

Once I was inside her office, my mother told me to close the door and take a seat. Guarded, I did as she asked. I kept quiet, waiting for her to talk first, even though I was curious about what she wanted with me.

Finally, she leaned back in her chair and began, "I know our training sessions didn't go well last semester. Considering the situation, I think we should still train, but differently this time."

"What do you mean?"

"We've gathered some intel on King Brikan during the summer break."

That made me curious. "What kind of intel?"

My mother shook her head. "I can't tell you that, but based on what we learned, I want to change your training. I want to train you with magic. A different kind of magic. It's dangerous, but I don't think we have a choice."

"You're being cryptic."

"I know. I'm sorry, but I can't reveal any more information."

I crossed my arms. "That doesn't make any sense. I'm the one he's after; I'm the one who will probably have to face him someday. You should be telling me everything, so I'm prepared."

Her hazel eyes narrowed, considering. "I'll tell you more when you come for training."

Was that bait to get me to come to training? It was working. "Fine!"

"Good. Then meet me at the top of this building's south turret next Saturday at midnight."

I stared at her. Why wait until Saturday? That was almost a week from now. And at midnight, at the top of a turret? It all sounded so suspicious. But now I was freaking curious.

"I'll be there."

"Good. Now you can go," she said. "Classes start tomorrow, and there will be many challenges this semester. Be ready."

For a moment, my heart squeezed. Was my mother being nice because she was worried about me? But then, as usual, she broke the spell by waving her hands at me, shooing me out of her sight.

Rolling my eyes, I got up and exited her office.

Out through the back of the building, I stopped and stared at the blackthorn tree for a moment. The tall, thick tree stood in the middle of the courtyard, right in the center of the academy. It was black and full of thorns. No green, no leaves. Last semester, it had given me a piece of its enchanted wood, with which I was able to craft a Dawnblade, the special sword the Blackthorn Hunters used to kill demons. But mine was even more special, because there was only one other like it in the rest of the world: the headmaster's first Dawnblade.

More than that, my Dawnblade was special to me because Rey had helped me forge it. He had even imbued it with his magic.

I shook my head and resumed my walk to the Gardenia building. It had taken me all summer to stop thinking about Rey. I wouldn't start now because I was back at the academy.

I turned the corner of the Statice building and gasped as something wet and warm washed over me. I halted and looked down at my arms.

They were covered in blood.

My stomach twisted, and horror rushed through me.

What was this? What was going on?

Laughter reached my ears and I looked to my left. A group of students, mostly males, laughed at me. One of them, a tall young man whose name I didn't remember, held an empty jar, smeared with blood.

"What the hell?" I asked as the blood dripped down my hair and stained my shirt.

"How is it to bathe in demon blood?" the guy asked with a snicker.

My stomach turned. This sticky red substance covering my arms and clothes and hair was demon blood?

"It's appropriate," a girl muttered, smiling.

"That's what you deserve," the first guy said with a snicker. "Mongrel."

The others laughed.

And I fumed.

It was one thing to insult me, to walk by me and bump my shoulder as if I was a nobody, but to throw blood on me? That was a new low.

I curled my sticky hands into fists, ready to punch the guy's teeth out. Instead, my magic flared up.

It was okay. I would burn his ass and he would cry in pain for the rest of the semester.

I took a step forward and—

An arm appeared in front of me, blocking my way.

"What's going on here?"

My magic faded from my veins as I stared at Rey standing a few inches from me.

The other students grew serious.

"Nothing," the guy said, his voice low.

Rey snatched the jar from the guy's hand and sniffed at it. "Demon blood. You're in big trouble, Tom."

That was the guy's name. Tom. I remembered seeing him in second-year classes before, which meant he was a third-year student now, like me.

Tom sized up Rey. "Just because you're a professor now doesn't mean you can boss us around."

Rey's body went rigid. "You want to bet? As soon as I walk away, I'll report you to the headmaster. I bet he won't appreciate his students harassing each other."

"I can't get in trouble again," a girl whispered.

"If you don't want to get into trouble, I suggest you never do something like this again," Rey said. "Now get out of my face before I change my mind."

The students scurried away.

And I stood there, completely at a lost for two reasons: One, Rey had let them walk away as if they had teased me with mild curses, and two, I was suddenly left alone with Rey at the edge of the Gardenia building.

Letting out a long breath, Rey turned to me. "I should have written them up."

I swallowed my shock and braced myself. "Why didn't you?"

Rey's gray eyes met mine. What a scene. I was there, dripping with smelly, sticky blood and standing in front of my perfect man. As a professor at the academy, Rey was dressed in a black suit—clothes similar to the male students' uniform, but without the tie. And instead of a white shirt, Rey's was black.

And underneath that shirt was the mark of the twin soul bond. The same one stamped an inch above my left breast.

Rey and I shared the soul bond. He was my soulmate. But he didn't want anything to do with me.

I took a step back, in need of space.

Rey's brows curled down. "Things are already on shaky ground with the half-bloods being outed. Classes haven't even started yet and people are already causing trouble. If I wrote them up now, it would only make everything worse."

"So what? I deserved being splashed with demon blood? And called ... what was it that Tom said?"

"Mongrel," Rey muttered.

"Yeah. That word. I know it means a mix of races, but why did it sound so dirty coming from his mouth?"

"Because it's supposed to be a derogatory word for half-bloods."

I shook my head. "Hell, I had just arrived and things are already exploding."

Rey's eyes turned a dangerous silver. "What is it? What else happened?"

What did he care? "It's none of your business."

He stilled once more, lifting his chin. He was so freaking handsome, even when looking at me with his usual coldness. My heart squeezed as I took him in—the sharpness of the angles of his face, the full lips, the bright eyes, the dirty blond hair that had grown a little since the last time I had seen him. The square set of his shoulders, the tall, lean frame of his hard body.

This handsome man was my soulmate.

But he didn't want me.

"You're right," he said in a low voice. "It's not."

Why did those words hurt more than I expected?

My head raised high, I walked past him and into the Gardenia building. I passed some female students, and they all stared at me. Some were quiet, but others either gasped in horror, whispered nasty things, or laughed as if it was funny.

Dying for a shower, I headed into my bedroom. Thankfully, Claire had dropped my things in there, but she was gone, probably organizing her things in her own bedroom.

All I wanted was to throw myself on my bed, hug my pillow, and fight the tears that burned behind my eyes. But because I would get my bed dirty, I simply sat down on the floor, curled my shoulders forward, and let a few tears fall.

What a great first day back. I couldn't wait to see what the rest of the semester had in store for me.

2

REY

DREADING the next hour of my life, I opened the door of the classroom. In the next few minutes, students would fill up the seats, and I would teach my first class at the academy.

And Erin would be among these students.

I had acted like a possessive boyfriend yesterday, but I hadn't meant to. It was by luck—or unluck—that I was leaving my office and witnessed Tom and his snob friends throw demon blood on her and call her that word. My blood had boiled, and I almost ripped his head off.

After I scared them off, I had wanted to take care of her, to help her to her dorm, to make sure she was okay, to help her with all that nasty blood, but I couldn't. I had made myself clear last semester, and now I had to maintain that facade. Besides, her mother's threat still hung over my head. I was sure she hadn't forgotten about it.

More than that, I was now a professor. Having feelings and getting involved with a student was against school rules. If I was caught, I would be fired.

And with Professor Crimson's threat to hurt Erin, I couldn't be fired yet.

Erin had no idea, but I had kept an eye on her during the summer. I told myself it was only to make sure Crimson wouldn't act while I wasn't paying attention. But deep down, I knew it was because I wanted to check on her, to make sure she was all right, that she was safe. Because I needed to see her with my own eyes.

When she and Claire went out one night and joined the treasure hunt, I longed to participate. It had been Erin's birthday, and just for one night, for one measly fucking night, I wished I could let go of all pretense. I wished I could hug her, wish her a happy birthday, and show her how much I loved her.

But that was my traitorous heart speaking.

There were so many obstacles separating us; it would be impossible to be together.

Even with the soul bond linking us.

This fucking soul bond. If this mark wasn't imprinted on my chest, everything would be easier.

Ava and her friends, Stella and Ruby, were the first ones to arrive in the classroom. Ava shot me a mild glare before taking a seat right in the middle. I frowned, returning my gaze to the books on my desk. Ever since she started at the academy, Ava had been a bitch in capital letters. But last semester, while she was looking for Harvey with Erin and me, I thought she wasn't so bad. And that her friends, the same ones who were seated with her now, weren't really her best friends.

Apparently, I was mistaken.

Other students arrived, including Peter and Harvey. Then, I saw Harper arrive alone.

With less than a minute to spare, Erin walked in, followed closely by Claire. Erin didn't even look my way as she took a seat in the back. Better this way. If she ignored me, it would be easier for me to ignore her too.

Although, I wondered how her previous evening had been. Had it been hard to scrub the blood from her hair? Had she slept well, or was she still having nightmares about her half-sisters?

I shook my head, pushing those thoughts away.

I waited another minute, then started my class: advanced combat. It wasn't a new class, but I had changed its curriculum. Thankfully, Randall didn't seem to care what I did with it.

Before, it had been mostly martial arts combat, but more advanced since it was only taught to the third and fourth years. However, I felt like that wasn't enough. So, I divided the class in two parts: theory and practice. For the first twenty minutes, we met in one of the lecturing halls in the Hyacinth building, which housed the combat training rooms and the gym. During this time, we would talk about combat techniques and strategies. We would even study the wars between the supernaturals and humans, and understand the tactics and why side X lost and side Y won.

I hoped that by studying the theory, the students wouldn't rush into a fight without a plan. I wanted to give them the means to come up with a plan even if they had thirty seconds to do so.

I hoped Erin would absorb the information and use it when she had to face King Brikan.

But she wasn't just ignoring me; she was also ignoring my class.

She had propped her legs up on the empty seat in front of

her, and she had the magical spells book open, instead of demon history, which was the one I was using to talk about the wars.

Every few minutes, she let out a long breath and glanced at her nails, or out the window, as if she was bored.

Was she trying to get under my skin?

She was succeeding.

At the end of the lecture part, I asked the students to write down what they expected from my class on a piece of paper, and pass it along to the front so I could collect them and read them later.

"All right," I said as I took the stack of paper back to my desk. "Please, get up and cross the hall to the combat classroom. You don't need to take your things."

For the next forty minutes, we would focus on the practical part. There would be days when I showed them some complicated moves and they had to replicate them, but for the most part, I would divide the class into teams and give them a challenge. They would have to come up with a plan of action.

I hoped it would be a fun class.

But so far, it had been tense as hell.

The students got to their feet and filed out of the classroom, going across the hall. Erin and Claire were last. So I wouldn't look at her, I turned my attention to the papers in my hand. I shuffled through them until I came upon a mostly blank sheet of paper.

"Erin," I called out before I could really think.

She halted and turned to me, her usually bright golden eyes sporting a cold shine. "Yes?"

I waited until Claire walked out, then pointed to the blank paper. "You didn't do the assignment."

"Oh, but I did," she said.

I frowned. "No, you didn't. I asked you to write down at least three things you expect from my class this semester. There's only your name here."

"That's the thing, *professor*." She drawled out the last word, as if it hurt her to say it. To be fair, it fucking hurt to hear her say it like that. "I don't expect anything."

Her sentence was arrogant, but her voice, her eyes were sad.

In shock, I stared as she dragged her feet across the hallway and joined the other students. Fuck, this wasn't going well. I knew being her professor wouldn't be easy, but I hadn't imagined it would be this hard.

And this was just the first day. How could I handle an entire semester like this?

I would worry about that later. Now I had to finish teaching this fucking class.

The students were gathered in a circle in the middle of the mat, waiting for me. I walked into the circle and told them what we would do next. "I've hidden three small flags in this classroom." The students looked around, trying to locate the flags. The classroom was simple—with the mat, the mirrored wall, a few pictures on the other walls, and a shelf full of weapons. There weren't many places to hide the flags in here. "Three different colors. I'll divide you into three teams and assign you a color. You and your team need to find your flag and protect it while capturing the other flags. The first team with their flag and an enemy flag wins."

Harvey nodded his head and Peter rolled his shoulders, both clearly pumped up for the game. Claire turned green and Ava rolled her eyes. And Erin glanced at her nails again.

I swear, she was doing it on purpose to irk me. That had to be it.

I divided the students into three groups. Ava and Harper ended up in one team, Peter and Claire ended up in another one, and Harvey and Erin were in the last one.

Then the game began.

Though some fighting happened, the game was supposed to be more about tactics and planning. Despite her aversion to martial arts and combat, Claire was clearly trying.

Unlike her friend, who stood by the window as if nothing was happening. Erin didn't lift a finger during the entire forty minutes.

But her team won because Harvey had been way too fast and stolen the flag from Peter, while still holding on to his.

"All right," I said, calling everyone. "Well done. You're dismissed."

Smiling and chatting about the game—apparently they all had fun—the students crossed the corridor to the lecture hall to collect their books and bags.

Erin lagged behind, as if she hadn't even seen the game had ended.

"Hey, let's go," Claire called her.

Erin blinked. "Oh, right."

She started walking in the direction of the door.

All right, I couldn't take this. "Erin," I called her again. "We need to talk."

Crossing her arms, Erin halted and faced me, her expression deadpan. "Yes, professor?"

"I'm ..." Claire started. She pointed to the door. "I'll wait in the other classroom." Like a scared, little mouse, Claire scurried out of the room.

I let out a slow breath. "Care to explain why you didn't participate in the game?"

She stared at me, her chin defiant, but the gleam in her eyes betrayed her bravado. "Because I didn't want to."

"This is a class," I said, trying to remain calm. "You know everything is graded. If you arrive on time, if you do the assignments, if you participate in class, and if you do well. So far, I can say you only have a good mark for arriving on time, and even that one was just barely."

"I think we both know I don't want to be in your class."

I nodded. "Unfortunately, it's a required class if you want to move on to the fourth year. And you need to pass it with good grades, otherwise it doesn't count. To get good grades, you need to participate."

Her nostrils flared. Erin was getting angry, and all I could think about was how I wanted to erase the distance between us and hug her, and tell her that it didn't matter, that we would get through it together. Even when her golden eyes flamed and her pink lips pouted in anger, she looked gorgeous. Her long black hair was pulled back into a loose braid, and the black combat uniform hugged her body, showing off the tempting curves of her body.

A man had only so much control.

"I don't care," she snapped. "Fail me if you have to, but I won't participate. You can't make me."

A sliver of anger snaked through my veins. She was really testing me here. "Erin—"

"Don't Erin me." She dropped her arms and clenched her fists. "We've been over this, haven't we?"

I swallowed the retort that flew to the tip of my tongue. "I'm your professor," I said, more for myself than for her. "You can't talk to me like that. Show me some respect."

Her eyes bugged and she pulled back as if I had slapped her. "You've got to be kidding me."

"That's it." I went to the corner of the classroom, opened the drawer from one of the cabinets, and pulled out a form. I filled it out and handed it to her. "Here. A disciplinary action for your behavior."

She only stared at the paper. "You mean, like detention? No way ..."

I walked to her, grabbed her hand, and shoved the form in her hand. "Don't make things worse."

Eyes still wide, Erin shook her head. "I don't know you anymore," she whispered, before whirling on her heels and marching away.

Once she was gone, I let out a deep breath and ran a hand through my hair. Holy fuck, this was going to be one long, long semester.

3

ERIN

I CRUMPLED the disciplinary action in my hand as I walked out of the classroom, wishing I could smother my rage like that too.

Detention? Really?

"What happened?" Claire asked. She had waited for me in the lecture hall, holding both her tote and mine.

"This." I handed her the crumpled note and picked up my tote.

She smoothed the paper and read it. "What? Why?"

Because he couldn't let me ignore his class. Didn't he realize it would be much easier on both of us if I pretended I wasn't there? Now he was giving me detention for it.

"Because he's a jerk," I muttered. "Come on. I have a pitstop before we go to our next class."

"A pitstop?" Claire followed me out the classroom. "Where?"

"My mother's class," I told her.

Either Claire guessed what I wanted with my mother, or she assumed it was better not to ask, because she remained quiet as we exited the Hyacinth building and walked to Orchid, where both my mother's class and our next class were located.

During Rey's class, the other students hadn't bothered me as much, but out here? I couldn't take three steps without hearing whispers, or seeing someone staring at me with disgust.

I heard the word "mongrel" as we walked into the building and I flinched.

"Ignore them," Claire whispered to me. She had been saying that so often, it sounded like her new motto.

"I'm trying," I whispered back. I turned to the right, where my mother's class was located. Claire didn't follow me. "Aren't you coming?"

"Your mother scares me almost as much as my father." She offered me a small smile. "If you don't mind, I'll go to our class and save a seat for you."

I nodded. Claire sauntered to the left, walking to our next class.

And I marched to the opposite side of the building. My mother's classroom was one of the biggest in the building, located near the south entrance.

As I expected, she was inside the classroom, looking over her notes at her desk, while students slowly filled the room. To call her attention, I knocked on the door twice.

She raised her head and her brows slammed down the moment she saw me. With sure steps, she approached me. "What is it?"

"Professor Martha, can we talk for a minute?" I asked while a few students walked by us. Only a handful of people knew she was my mother, and we wished to keep it that way. If I was having a hard time because of my heritage, imagine what she would get if people found out she had fallen in love with King Brikan once.

She gestured to the corner of the corridor, where it opened to a foyer in front of the south doors. Once we rounded the corner, she crossed her arms. "What is this about?"

"I want to transfer out of Rey Lowe's class."

"*Professor* Rey," she corrected me. "He's your professor now."

"Not for long if you let me transfer." As my advisor, all changes to my schedule had to be approved by her.

"You can't transfer. This is a required class to move on to the fourth year. If you plan on graduating, you have to take this class now."

"But ..." I stopped myself.

"But what?"

My mother didn't know anything about Rey and me. She had seen us kiss the first time, and I had no idea what she made of that, but she didn't know about the soul bond and everything else that had happened between us since then.

She didn't know I loved him.

"Tell me another professor teaches this class."

My mother shook her head once. "No. This class was taught by Professor Genevieve before, but now only Professor Rey teaches it. You have to take this class, Erin."

I groaned. "You know as well as I do that there's a chance I'll never graduate." If my father came after me, I was done for. I would never finish the academy program.

"We're doing everything we can to change that, aren't we? We'll find a way of defeating the supreme demon. After that, you'll wish you had taken all the right classes to graduate and become a full-fledged demon hunter."

I frowned. Honestly, I hadn't thought that far ahead. Did I want to become a demon hunter? What were my other options? Move to Chasseur Ville, open a store, and live peacefully? That sounded awfully tempting.

"What if I don't want to become a member of the Blackthorn Hunters?"

My mother's hazel eyes blazed. "This is not up for discussion, Erin. You're taking the advanced combat class. That's final." She glanced at her wristwatch. "Now if you'll excuse me, my class is about to start."

Turning her back to me, my mother walked back into her classroom, and I leaned against the wall, defeated. I thought it was a damn done deal. That my mother would have no problem transferring me out of Rey's class.

I clenched my fists, feeling more pissed than before.

But if I didn't move now, I would miss my next class. I would get a bad mark, and that would make me even angrier.

Letting out a long, calming breath, I pushed off the wall. Movement outside the glass doors caught my attention.

I approached the doors and glanced out. To the left of the entrance, an older, tall man with thick blond hair loomed over Ava.

"You're close to disappointing me, Ava," the man said. Though his voice was muted by the closed doors, I was sure he was yelling at her. "Do not disappoint me, or you'll regret it."

"I'm trying!" she shouted back. "But your expectations are hard to achieve."

"You're wrong." He shook his head once. "You're my daughter. You can achieve anything."

Ava rolled her eyes. "You're asking too much of me."

The man clenched his fists and inched over her, as if he was trying to stop himself from hitting her.

I could help with that.

I pulled one of the doors open and walked out. "There you are, Ava."

She stared at me with momentary shock, though her father glared at me. "So, it is true. You're associating with scum."

I glanced around, unfazed. "Who are you talking about, sir?"

"I won't stoop to your level." The man glared at me, before turning to Ava. "I know you have class starting in two minutes, so I won't keep you. But you've been warned, Ava. Do not disappoint me."

After another disgusted glance at me, Ava's father strutted away.

The blond bitch looked at me. "Why did you do that?"

I shrugged. "I don't know. But aren't you glad I did?"

She scoffed but didn't answer me. Instead, she walked up to me and the both of us entered the building again. In silence, we started down the corridor, going to our class before we were too late.

Fifteen seconds later, Ava spoke up. "That was my father."

"I got that part."

"You know how Professor Eleanor is with Harvey? My father is ten times worse than that with me. He expects greatness from me, and he's upset I've been hanging out with you."

"But you haven't. Not much."

"But it was enough," she said, sounding rather sad. "Tom told my father. You know Tom? I heard he threw demon blood on you yesterday."

"Yeah, I know who he is." That damn blood … I had spent hours in the shower last night to get it off me.

She grimaced. "I'm sorry for what he did to you."

I stared at her, confused. Why was she apologizing? "It wasn't your fault."

"I know, but … he's my cousin." She shrank into herself, seemingly ashamed of the revelation.

Well, I didn't need to know that either, but it was nice to see she sort of cared. "It's okay. I get it. We don't choose family."

"Right." She nodded once. "He's a bastard. Always trying to get me in trouble." Her blue eyes shone bright. "I know. We could get back at him."

"You mean, like revenge?"

"Yes," she whispered, a tone of excitement in her voice. "Come on. I have some ideas."

Ava entered the classroom and sauntered to where Claire was seated. In shock, I watched as she left an empty seat beside Claire, but took the next one. She glanced at me and beckoned me over.

Claire stared at me, puzzled, while Ruby and Stella, who were seated on the other side of the classroom, seemed to be as shocked as I was.

"Miss Delman?" Professor Astrid called me. Last semester, I had weapon forging class with her, but this semester I had demonic lairs. "Class starts in ten seconds. I suggest you come inside before I have to give you a bad mark."

"Yes, professor," I said, striding inside.

I sat down between Claire and Ava. Claire grabbed my arm. "What's going on?"

I shook my head and whispered, "I'm not really sure."

AVA COULD BE CONFUSED as one of my best friends during our demonic lairs class. Whenever Professor Astrid wasn't looking, or when she told us to read a chapter by ourselves before discussion, Ava took the opportunity to lean over my desk to plan the prank on her cousin.

As much as I wanted revenge, I didn't want to go overboard and break any more rules—I already had a long list of reasons to be expelled. I didn't want to add anything to it.

But I couldn't deny her idea had merit.

After class, instead of going to the cafeteria for lunch, Ava, Claire, and I headed to the underground garage. According to Ava, Tom had gotten a new car before classes started, a super fancy one, and he kept visiting the freaking thing to show it off to his friends.

As Ava suspected, Tom was right there, beside his blue and silver convertible, seated on the hood, while his friends surrounded him and examined the car.

He had a superior air around him, as if he was seated on a throne and his friends were his subjects.

I hated people like that.

"Told you he would be here," Ava whispered.

I spied from around the stairs, where we were hiding. "Are you two ready?"

Claire shook her head, but Ava nodded. She pulled out her cell phone, which she shouldn't be carrying, and set the camera on video mode. She was going to record it all.

I got why Claire was apprehensive, but I had to side with Ava on this one. The freaking dude had thrown nasty demon blood on me! He deserved to burn in hell.

That was a little too much for me, so I would burn his car instead.

Or pretend to.

I called my magic and let it fill my veins. Then I sent it to Tom's car. I wasn't sure what I was doing; I was trying to mimic when I conjured fake zombies, but this time, it was fake fire.

Closing my eyes for a second, I focused on my magic and what I wanted it to do. A moment later, smoke rose from under the car.

"What the fuck?" Tom yelled, hopping off the hood. He took two steps back, his friends along with him.

The smoke grew thicker and darker.

"Is there a fire?" one of his friends asked. "I don't see it."

Tom crouched down and tried spying under the car. "I don't see it either." Then he opened the car's hood. A thick cloud of smoke greeted him, and he stepped back again, coughing as if the smoke was real. "What the hell is going on?"

Now, for the final show. The smoke turned into fire. Tall, orange flames licked the car, enveloping it.

"No! My car!" Tom knelt on the ground, his hands buried in his hair. "My poor car!" Tears came down his face.

"He's crying," Ava whispered. "Oh my gosh, he's really crying."

"Isn't that enough?" Claire asked. "He's already terrified for his car. You got your revenge. Now let's go before we're found out."

But it was so much fun to see him suffering.

The smoke and fire were fake, but his desperation wasn't. When he realized it was all pretend, he would be mortified that he had acted like a baby in front of his friends.

I willed my magic to work for another five minutes, then dropped my hands. "All right. I'm done. We can go."

Claire was the first one to climb up the steps.

Ava and I lingered for a few more seconds before following her.

Once we were on the main level and heading to the cafeteria, Ava let out a content squeal. "That was great." She patted the pocket of her jacket, where her phone was stashed. "And now we've got a video of Tom crying like a baby over his car." She snorted. "If someday he gets married, I'll show this video to his fiancée. He'll be even more humiliated."

I chuckled, but it wasn't heartfelt. I felt better after pranking Tom, but at the same time, I didn't feel like it fixed anything. I got my revenge, but it didn't bring me peace.

Now I understood why people said revenge wasn't worth it.

However, as I glanced at Ava, who practically skipped at my side, I wondered if there was something this prank had brought me.

Maybe a new friend?

It was too early to tell, but I kind of liked the idea of Ava not being an enemy anymore.

4

REY

AFTER THE SECOND day of school, I headed to the Aster building.

When I first got Randall's note early that morning, I thought he was asking for me, and my mind spun. What could he want? He hadn't called me, or Erin for that matter, ever since the big ordeal at the Spring Hunter Ball last semester. We both still had contracts with him, but he seemed to have forgotten about us. He hadn't even asked us to continue searching for the half-demons to join his Black Knight Unit. Could he want something else now?

But as the day went on, I learned others had been called to the meeting. What the fuck could this be about?

I tried focusing on my classes during the day, but it was hard when two topics filled every inch of my brain. There was a meeting, which made me uneasy, and then there was Erin.

I hadn't seen her all day, and despite wanting to feel relieved about it, it only made me anxious. Many students and professors and staff had showed discontent about having the half-demons in the school, and Erin was a double negative since she wasn't only half-demon, but she also was a demonic princess. I had stopped Tom and his friends from doing worse things to her two days ago, but since then, I had heard whispers about how they wished she was gone.

Or dead.

To make things worse, yesterday's argument between Erin and me brought knots to my stomach. I fucking hated fighting with her. I hated that now I was her professor and we had to act all respectful and distant. Well, in a way, that was better, since I needed to stay away from her, but it still bothered me anyway.

The way she poked at me ... it both excited and bothered me. I had been so agitated, I had given her fucking detention. If I had stopped to think, I wouldn't have. Because now it meant she had to come to the classroom and spend time with me.

Alone.

I was in so much trouble.

Pushing those thoughts away, I picked up my things and went to the Aster building. When I entered the big meeting room across the hall from his office, I realized it was a school board meeting of sorts. Randall hadn't arrived yet, but everyone else was here. The senior professors—Crimson, Martha, Genevieve, and Graham—and a handful of seasoned demon hunters from the nearest outpost—including Alain Heyward, Ava's father.

I took my usual seat at the right of Randall's chair and waited in silence. Crimson was right in front of me, on the other side, and I tried hard not to look at him, lest it remind me of the threat he had made last semester. Because of this threat, I hadn't slept well in over four months.

Crimson tapped his fingers on the long, black table. "How

long will he keep us waiting?" he muttered, glancing at his wristwatch.

I knew what he was doing: stirring the pot.

Many of these professors and demon hunters were against the Black Knight Unit. They were already displeased with Randall. Crimson was only poking at the wound.

Whispers began anew and I frowned.

Moments later, Randall strolled into the meeting room and the whispers ceased.

"Sorry I'm late," he said. "I had an important call." He took his usual seat at the head of the table. His chair wasn't different from ours in any way, and yet he sat on it as if it was a throne. I guess being immortal and ridiculously powerful made you a being apart. "I tried having this meeting last week, but some of you couldn't make it, so we're doing this now."

"What is this about?" Crimson asked, his voice uninterested.

"To discuss plans for the upcoming semester," Randall said simply.

Alain crossed his arms. "I don't need to be here for this."

"No, but we can discuss something else, then," Professor Graham started. "The fact that Erin Delman and many other half-demons are walking around campus as if they belonged here."

Graham had been vocal last semester when Erin was found out and almost expelled from the school. Apparently, his opinion hadn't changed.

"I agree," Alain said. "Talking about those half-demons is more important than deciding on the school's agenda."

Crimson nodded. "We need to eradicate the half-demons."

I gritted my teeth. Oh, so help me. It would be a miracle if I got through this meeting without either starting a fight or murdering someone.

Alain and Graham agreed instantly, along with the other demon hunters in the room. Professor Genevieve was oddly quiet, but Professor Martha didn't stay silent.

"That's ridiculous," she protested. "They shouldn't be blamed for their heritage. It's not their fault."

"Then we find their parents and punish them too," Graham suggested.

I curled my hands under the table, trying to hold my tongue. Three people in here knew I was half-demon. If the others found out, I would be shunned too. Maybe even fired, and I couldn't let that happen yet.

"As one of the leaders of the Blackthorn Hunters, I propose we lock all the half-demons up." Fingers steepled, Alain leaned over the table. "After that, we conduct public executions, as a warning to other half-demons who think they can infiltrate our society."

Martha gasped. "That's barbaric."

Alain shrugged. "Then let's have trials. I'm sure they would be convicted anyway."

"Convicted of what?" Martha asked, clearly losing her patience. "Of trying to adapt to a world that doesn't want them? I'll repeat; they aren't guilty of who they are."

Graham glared at Martha. "Why are you defending them?"

"Enough," Randall said, his voice low but powerful. Final. Everyone in the room quieted. "I didn't call you here to talk about the half-demons and the Black Knight Unit, but if you insist, let me tell you bluntly: They are here to stay."

"That's preposterous!" Graham barked.

"You think so," Randall said, remaining as calm and regal as ever. "But you forget that I'm the first demon hunter, the founder of the Blackthorn Hunters and the Blackthorn Hunters Academy, and the current headmaster. My word is law. And I say the half-demons stay. In fact, not only are they staying, but they are also joining us. The half-demons who are of age will enroll in the academy immediately and attend classes as students."

"You can't be serious," Alain said, his eyes wide.

"What if I refuse to teach them?" Graham asked, defiant.

"Then you'll be fired," Randall said with a snarl. "Let it be known: You and all the other academy staff are to treat all the half-demons students with respect, just as you would a demon hunter student. If you don't, it's your job on the line."

Graham punched the table hard, but swallowed whatever curse he wanted to throw at Randall.

"Randall, you know you're practically starting a civil war, right?" Alain asked, his voice dangerously low.

"It's a war only if you make it one," Randall said, unconcerned. "Now that this issue is resolved, can we talk about the school schedule?"

The professors, demon hunters, and the rest of the staff weren't pleased about the decision, but no one protested. No one dared go against Randall's wishes, at least, not right under his nose.

The tension in the room was palpable as the topic of the meeting shifted and we finally discussed the upcoming events, exams, the third-year midterm games, and such.

An hour later, Randall dismissed us. With unhurried steps, he was the first out of the room. As usual, he holed up in his office.

Graham, Alain, and the others who were opposed to

Randall's plan got together at the end of table. They discussed in hushed tones, but anyone could see they weren't happy about the headmaster's decision. They'd be fucking stupid to fight Randall head-on.

Professor Martha shot a glare at them, then turned to me. She paused beside me and said in a whisper, "Erin asked to be excused from your class." She turned her hazel eyes to me. "What did you do?"

Fuck, what had Erin told her mother? "Nothing that I'm aware."

"I gather you heeded my words and are staying away from her?"

Everyone was so serious and fucking sinister today.

"I teach her class, you know. But other than that, I'm as far as I can get."

"Good," she said with a short nod. "Keep it that way."

Without another word, Martha marched out, as if she too had a plan and had to get on with it.

I exited the conference room before I couldn't exercise my self-control anymore and exploded on Graham and Alain, and trotted out the building. With my first step, I turned left, aiming for the Snapdragon building, still not used to the fact that my room wasn't there anymore. Now that I was a professor, I had been given a townhouse at Dahlia Villa on the other side of campus.

I whirled around to correct my lapse and found Crimson standing in my path.

"That meeting was enlightening," Crimson said. I slipped my hands in the pockets of my pants, doing my best to stay nonchalant while Crimson rambled on. "Didn't you think? Professor Graham and demon hunter Alain are ready to go against Randall. This is exactly what we needed."

"If you say so."

"Don't you get it?" Crimson's eyes widened with excitement. "This is an opportunity. The board is already against Randall's decision. If you push it, if you keep sowing seeds of discontentment throughout the school, if you—"

"Me?"

"Yes, you." The glint in Crimson's eyes darkened. "Or did you forget our deal?" He took a step closer and smiled at me. "I thought you would do anything to protect your soulmate."

My hands balled into fists inside my pockets, and I gritted my teeth. I wanted to punch him. Maybe if I hit him hard enough, his arrogance would fall out.

"What do you want me to do?" I asked, the words giving me a headache.

"Just keep an ear open," Crimson said. "Pay attention to people who seem unhappy with Randall's decisions. I want their names."

"Okay." I rolled my shoulders, in need of getting away from him. "Is that it?"

"Rey, I want to be headmaster by the end of this semester," Crimson said, his voice low. "You better find a way, otherwise ... poor Erin."

Losing my control, I closed the distance between us and loomed over him. "Stop threatening her. I'll do what you ask; just leave her alone."

A wide smile spread over Crimson's lips. "That's all I want." With a short nod of his head, he walked away.

I let out a long breath and started back to my townhouse, my mind reeling with half-baked plans. Crimson's deal was simple: I had to either kill Randall, or implicate him enough so he would be dismissed as the headmaster of the academy.

Then, Crimson would step in and take over. I had until the end of the semester to do that.

Otherwise, he would kill Erin.

Maybe I should kill Crimson instead. No, that was my many years as one of the underworld's pawns speaking. I wasn't like that anymore. Even if Crimson threatened Erin, I wouldn't kill him. I could hurt him very, very badly, but I wouldn't end his life. I didn't need his fucking blood on my hands.

No, I just needed to come up with a plan and fast, before Erin got hurt on my account.

5

ERIN

My first class of the day was demon anthropology. It wasn't as boring as it sounded, but since every student except for Claire and Harper kept looking at me as if I was a bug to be squashed, I couldn't focus on what the professor was saying.

After the prank on Tom, I thought Ava and I had broken through a barrier, but as soon as we went to the cafeteria, she left Claire and me to join her so-called friends, Stella and Ruby. I hadn't told Ava that when she went missing last semester, Stella and Ruby didn't seem one bit worried about it. Her friendships were none of my business.

Claire had forgotten about the prank and stayed with me all day, even when some nasty students walked by us, clearly trying to push me to the side, and bumped into me and called me names.

That word again.

Mongrel.

I had heard it before, of course, but never used in such a derogatory way.

It was ridiculous, but it bothered me to the core.

I shook my head and glanced out the windows. The sun was already high, shining bright over the blackthorn tree in the center of the courtyard. It would be another hot day at the academy.

When I returned my gaze to the front of the class, I caught sight of Harper. Alone as usual, she was seated a row below Claire and me, and a little to the left. She kept stealing glances at Claire, who was oblivious to Harper's feelings.

After what happened with Tanner, I didn't think Claire was ready to let anyone in yet, which was a shame, because it was stamped on Harper's face how much she liked Claire. I was sure Harper would treat Claire right.

Unlike a certain half-demon I knew.

And there it went. It didn't matter what was going on in my life, my thoughts always went back to Rey. What could I do? He was my freaking soulmate, even if he pushed me away.

Sometimes, I wished there was a way to break this damn soul bond.

Class ended and I barely noticed the time passing. Claire and I picked up our things and headed out along with the other students.

Once we exited the Orchid building, we heard yells and loud chatter. As a giant, curious mass, all the students moved toward the voices, Claire and I included. We rounded the corner of the Aster building and saw a lot of people standing in front of the main doors of the building, some holding signs protesting the half-demons at the school.

"What's going on?" I asked, trying to count how many people were there. At least two dozen. And they were all older than us. Among them, I saw Ava's father. Parents. These people were all parents.

"I don't know," Claire whispered.

Remi, one of the campus security guards, walked up to us, his hands open wide. "Stay back," he told us.

"What's going on?" a student asked. Several joined in the query, demanding explanations.

Remi shook his head. "The parents are protesting."

"What?" someone asked.

"This morning, headmaster Randall announced that the half-demons who are of age will be joining the academy as students," Remi told us. Loud chatter and protests started from all around me. "Stay back, please, or I'll have to use force. In fact, you should go to your next class before I report you all!"

Claire slipped her hand in mine. "Let's get out of here."

We weaved through the crowd until we were around the back of the building. "I feel personally attacked," I told her in a low voice as we walked by the side of the courtyard, going to the Gardenia building.

"You should." She glanced around. "I think that is just the beginning. If what Remi said is true, I fear things will only get worse."

I nodded. She was right. With this announcement, the headmaster had placed half-demons on the same level as the demon hunters. A lot of people would be furious.

We turned the corner of the Statice building, when a group converged on us.

"There you are," Tom said, walking up to me. "The most famous mongrel of all."

I puffed my chest. "What do you want, Tom?"

His friends surrounded Claire and me. Shit, this wasn't going to end well.

"Let's just say I learned you're the one who fake-burned

my car," he drawled. What? How? Had Ava told him? He went on, "Also, I'm sure you're the one who convinced the head-master to let the half-breeds into the academy."

"W-what?" I shrieked, because, well, how did he find out about the former, and how did he come up with a stupid idea for the latter? "That's ridiculous."

Tom poked at my arm. "Ridiculous is having your skinny ass parading across the academy as if you belong here."

"S-stop," Claire said, putting on a fake bravado. She didn't fool anyone with the tremor in her voice, her wide eyes, and the shake of her hands. "Erin didn't do anything wrong."

Tom turned a nasty smile toward Claire. "Are you a pure blood, Claire? If so, why are you associating with the likes of her?"

"Tom, we can talk about this," I started, fearing for my friend. "Just let Claire go, okay?"

He fixed his hard eyes on me. "Talk about this? No ... I'm gonna beat it out of you, and your friend here gets to watch."

"What?" A gasp ripped past my throat as hands closed around my arms, pulling them back.

Claire yelled, but someone grabbed her and pulled her back. Both of us were dragged to the side of the Gardenia building, behind the tall bushes and thick trees. The only way to be found was to scream, but would anyone come? For a half-demon? For a demonic princess?

I doubted it.

Tom came at me and punched my stomach.

I gasped as the air flew out of my lungs and pain spread through my torso.

Holy shit.

On instinct, I called my magic. I rejoiced in the feeling of power as it traveled up and down my veins.

"Stop it!" Claire yelled.

Ready to punch me again, Tom hesitated.

And I dropped my magic.

If I fought back, if I used my magic on them, if I ended up hurting Tom and his friends, it would only make things worse. The ones against the half-demons would have proof that we were unstable and disturbed and angry, or whatever else they wanted to believe. Things would get blown out of proportion, and parents would have something to use against Randall's rule. The half-demons would be expelled or killed, and I would be among them.

So I braced myself when Tom pulled his arm back and punched me again.

The pain was excruciating.

I ended up calling my magic again, but instead of attacking, I used it as a defense mechanism. I used my magic to numb my muscles so I didn't feel as much pain while Tom punched my stomach and my face, and kicked my hips and my chest.

Like dead weight, I fell on the ground. No one was holding me now. There was no reason to. Even if I hadn't been using my magic to shield the pain, I was sure I would be numb from being beaten.

But as it was, I was too weak to hold the magic. I could feel it rearing back and the pain spreading over my entire body.

Tom straddled me, his face inches from mine. "Now, you get what you deserve, you mongrel bitch." His Dawnblade appeared in his hand.

Despair swirled in my chest. "W-what ...?" I tried asking what the hell he was going to do, but the words got stuck in my throat.

"Say hi to your daddy." Tom lifted his sword high.

The next second, he was on the ground beside me.

Harvey flew over me and landed a roundhouse kick to Tom's face. "What the hell is wrong with you?"

I saw Peter, Ava, and Harper joining Harvey in pushing Tom and his friends back, before Claire leaned over me, blocking everything else. "Are you okay?"

"D-dandy," I croaked.

She hooked her arm around mine and tugged. "Can you stand?"

I tried shaking my head, but that only brought on more pain. I tried calling my magic again, but I was too weak, too hurt to have control over it.

"Get out of my way before I kill you too," Tom yelled from somewhere behind Claire.

"It was me, you idiot," Ava shouted back. "It was me who pranked you and your car. You just beat an innocent person."

"Innocent?" Tom snapped. "She's a fucking half-demon. There's nothing innocent about her."

"Get out of here, man, before I beat you up," Harvey warned.

"Let them come," Peter said. "I would love to kick their asses."

They argued more, but my mind was so out of it, it was hard to follow their exchange. But when they all surrounded me, I gathered they had been successful in getting rid of Tom and his gang.

Ava knelt beside me. "We'll take you to the infirmary."

"No," Claire protested. "Cecile is against the half-demons too." Cecile was the campus physician. She had always been so kind to me. Could she really hate half-demons too? Would she start treating me badly because I wasn't like her?

"Then what?" Harper asked. "We take her to her dorm and treat her pain and wounds with ibuprofen?"

Claire shook her head. "I know where we can take her."

I wasn't sure if I had heard Claire's plan, if I had dreamed it, or if I had missed it completely. All I knew was that suddenly I was in Harvey's arms. To avoid being seen, he carried me around the back of the dorms, the Hyacinth building, and the training arena, all the way to Dahlia Villa, on the other side of campus.

I was sure they were delivering me to my mother when Harvey climbed the front porch steps of a townhouse and Claire knocked on the door.

"No," I croaked. "She'll finish killing me."

"It's not a she," Ava whispered to me.

A moment later, the door flew open and Rey stared at us, his gray eyes wide and enraged. "What the fuck happened?"

"Tom and his friends beat her up," Claire said.

"It's my fault," Ava said.

"It doesn't matter," Claire continued. "All that matters is that they almost killed her and they saved her." She gestured to Harvey, Peter, and Harper. I was sure she was leaving Ava out of it on purpose.

"We wanted to take her to the infirmary—"

"It's good that you didn't," Rey said, interrupting Harvey. "Cecile hates the half-demons."

Claire nodded. "That's what I said."

Finally, Rey's eyes found mind. A gentle shine covered them, giving them an almost silver glow. He stepped to my side and slid his arms under me. "Give her to me. I'll take care of her." Harvey let go, and suddenly, I was in Rey's arms.

Despite the pain and numbness, I felt self-conscious. I

tried holding my head up, or recoiling into myself. This was too much. The less I touched him, the better.

Rey took a step back and Claire advanced with him. "I'll help you."

"No," Rey said, almost too quickly. "You all should go back to class right now before this gets blown out of proportion. With Randall's announcement, things will be crazy for a while, and you all should act as normal as possible to avoid problems."

He had to do some convincing, but finally my friends left.

And Rey carried me inside his townhouse.

6

REY

HOLDING her gently so I wouldn't hurt her anymore, I took Erin to my bedroom on the second floor. Although the townhouse had been given to me a month ago, I barely had any furniture here. The only bed in the house was mine.

So that was where I laid her.

She sank into the mattress with a long sigh and closed her eyes.

Holy fuck ... my chest tightened as I looked at her. There were two purpling marks on her cheeks, a scratch on her chin, and she had a split lip. With trembling hands, I sat beside her and unbuttoned her white shirt. This was the first time I had seen Erin without a shirt, and despite the thrill that seeing her lace white bra over her plump breasts should have given me, my stomach sank at the sight of the red marks right above her chest, and on her stomach.

Channeling my magic, I hovered a hand over her bruises and checked if there was more damage hidden on the inside. My magic was dark and far from having healing properties, but I was sure that if something was wrong, I would know. My magic didn't spike, which made me believe her bruises were all external. With the right amount of rest and pain medicine, she would be fine.

Unlike my heart, which was being ripped to shreds right now.

Holy fuck.

This was torture.

Seeing her like this was torture. The rage in my veins spiked, and I clenched my fists. I wanted to go after the responsible ones right this instant and kill them with my own hands.

But I also wanted to hold her, to care for her, to heal her, to make sure she was forever safe.

I scoffed. I had been so afraid Crimson would be the one to hurt her, but so sure he wouldn't because he needed me that I had lowered my guard. Look where that had gotten me.

I hated myself.

I stared at her some more, at how her chest seemed to be moving up and down in a slow fashion. She was sleeping. I wanted to wake her up to make sure she was okay, to give her some medicine, but she seemed so hurt and out of it, perhaps it was best if she slept.

I reached up and smoothed her long black hair away from her face. Her beautiful face was marred by bruises. My rage stirred again and I clenched my teeth, trying to keep it in. Exploding now would only make everything worse.

I pulled my hand back and noticed her clothes were dirty and the sleeve of her jacket was ripped. I would need to get her some clean clothes, but for now, I could make her more comfortable.

Gently, I removed her boots and socks and covered her up to the waist with my blanket.

I had imagined Erin in my bed many, many times, but in my head, she had been smiling and happily writhing under me. Never in a million years would I have thought she would end up in my bed in this situation.

With a long sigh, I rose from the bed and went to the kitchen downstairs, where I hunted for some medicine and made chamomile tea. I didn't know when she would wake up, but I wanted to have it ready for her. I remembered having some magical healing herbs stored in the pantry. I picked some up and put them in the tea. That would accelerate the healing process.

I glanced at my phone, which had been charging in the kitchen. It wasn't even noon yet. Erin had two more classes this afternoon. I hoped Claire would tell their professors that Erin was sick, because if I contacted them, it would look suspicious.

I also had one class to teach this afternoon. If Erin remained sleeping, I could go, but I certainly didn't want to. Perhaps I too would lie that I wasn't feeling well, and then stay here with her.

Carrying a small tray with the medicine and the tea, I went back to my bedroom. Since I didn't have any other furniture upstairs, I put the tray on the floor beside the bed and sat on the edge of my bed.

Afraid Erin could have been more hurt than I thought, I rested my hand over her forehead. Her temperature seemed normal enough.

As if she had felt my touch, Erin stirred slightly. A moment later, she groaned. Next, she whimpered and her body jerked. She either was having one of those nightmares again, or she was remembering what had happened to her.

"Erin." I held her arms. "Wake up." She jerked against my hold, her head thrashing side to side as she uttered ineligible words. "Wake up, Erin."

"No!" she shouted.

In a flash, her eyes shot open and she scooted closer to the edge of the mattress. I held her wrist before she fell off the bed. "Careful." I smoothed my thumb over her skin. "You're okay now." Golden eyes on mine, her body sagged. "You're fine now."

She pressed her hand to her stomach and groaned. "What happened?" She glanced around. "Where am I?"

I frowned. "You don't remember?"

She shook her head once, but then her eyes widened and she inhaled a sharp breath. "Tom and his friends." She glanced down at herself. I hadn't buttoned up her shirt, and she pulled the blanket to cover herself. "Ow," she muttered before bringing her hand to her face.

"You must be hurting." I fluffed my pillows so she could rest against them, then grabbed the pain medicine and the cup of tea from the tray. "Here. Take this. It'll help with the pain."

Wary, Erin leaned back on the propped pillows and took the medicine and tea from me. She was visibly weak, but she resisted it well. "I thought I had been delirious."

"About?"

"Being brought here. You allowing me in." Averting her eyes, she took the medicine and drank some of the tea. She handed me the tea back and sat up. "I should go."

My body stiffened. "Go where? You're bruised and hurting. And don't think I can't see you're hanging on by a thread. Just lie down and rest."

She returned her eyes to mine, so raw it felt like a punch in the gut. "I don't want to be here."

Ouch.

"I understand that, but this is the best place for you right now." I stood and took a step back from the bed. "If you prefer, I can leave, but please, just stay here and rest for a while."

Erin shook her head. "Ow." She pressed her hands to her temples.

"See? You're still hurt." I took another step back. "Please go back to sleep."

Those golden eyes locked on mine. "For the record, I don't like this."

I nodded. "I know. It's fine. I'll leave you alone."

Her brows curled down. I thought she would say something else, but instead, she lay back on my pillows and rolled to her side. She groaned, probably from pain, and I had to hold myself back because my instinct was to run to her and ask what the problem was.

I exited the room and pulled the door until it was almost closed—I wanted to hear in case she called me—and went downstairs before I could break down and tell her how *I* was hurting for her.

Before I told her how much she meant to me.

***

Erin slept through the afternoon and evening. I didn't teach my class that day, but in the evening, I was itching to get out, though my reasons weren't noble.

I wanted to find the fucking bastard who had done this to Erin and break his face.

My mind told me to hang on and stay quiet about this, that if I did anything, it would mess everything up, but I couldn't stay still. My heart had been squeezed too fucking hard. It hurt too much, and I had to make someone pay for it.

I found Tom exiting one of the later classes in the Statice building with his friends. From there, he went to the cafeteria for dinner. I couldn't beat the crap out of him in public. I had to wait until later.

After dinner, Tom and his friends hung around the media room for a bit, then they went to their dorm rooms. I would have preferred to meet him outside, but if he wasn't coming, I would go inside and kick his ass right in his bedroom.

I was about to enter the lobby, when I saw Tom coming down the stairs. He had a cigarette and lighter in his hands. I scooted into the shadows and waited until he was out of the Snapdragon building, and had walked around the building so no one would see him.

He lit the cigarette.

And I rushed him.

Gasping, Tom dropped the cigarette and the lighter as I pushed him against the wall, pressing my forearm to his throat.

"You fucking bastard," I said through gritted teeth.

"W-what the ... fuck?" he tried speaking, but I pressed his throat more. As a demon hunter student, Tom had increased strength, so he pushed against me. But that was no match for my demon side.

"You deserve to die, do you know that?" I balled my free hand into a fist, ready to smash his face in.

"W-why?" he croaked, his eyes wide.

"You think beating up a half-demon is great? Think again!"

Tom's eyes widened. "Y-you're defending ... those mongrels?"

Red tinted my vision. I raised my fist.

And punched the wall, half an inch from Tom's face.

If it depended on me, I would have broken his nose, maybe even beaten him unconscious like he had done to Erin —or worse. But there were too many factors to consider here.

If I beat him up, he could report me to Randall, and I would be fired, no doubt. And if I was fired, I would have to leave. I had seen what could be done to Erin if I wasn't paying attention. What if I was far away? No, I had to stay.

Moreover, I didn't think Erin would forgive me for killing him. Even after what he did to her.

Because of that, I nearly broke my fingers on the stone wall instead of his pretty face.

"Be warned, bastard," I snarled, my face inches from his. "If you touch her again, if you even look at her, I'll kill you. Got it?"

Tom nodded, but didn't say anything. He didn't even look me in my eyes, the little shit.

I pressed him against the wall, making him gag, just to emphasize my warning, then I whirled and left before I regretted sparing his life.

I DIDN'T GO BACK to my townhouse that night. At least, not to stay. The most I did was leave some clothes for Erin outside the bedroom door—I had stopped by her dorm and gotten a clean uniform. After that, all I did was check to see if Erin was still inside and if she was doing okay, but I didn't go in. I only watched her through the window like a fucking creep.

I wanted to go to her. Every cell in my body pulled me to her as if she were a magnet. But I couldn't, I shouldn't.

Because if I did, if I found her in my bed, with her shirt half undone, with those big golden eyes watching me, expecting more of me ... I wouldn't be able to resist her.

I didn't want to sleep. My stamina was high, but the emotions of the day had worn me out. Exhaustion screamed through every nerve of my body. Once more, I itched to go back to my house, but I stayed put.

Instead, I went to my office in the Aster building. I lay on the small couch, my feet dangling over the arm, and tried to sleep. My mind raced, my heart squeezed, and my gut knotted every time I closed my eyes. I thought of Erin, of the way she had looked when her friends had brought her to me, of how I would have killed Tom if I had allowed myself.

I thought of how stupid I had been all this time, thinking I was keeping her safe. She was in more danger than I had realized. It wasn't only Crimson threatening her, or Randall's leash around our necks. It was all the others who were against the half-demons, all the others who wanted to execute the demonic princess. I had to watch out for them.

I had to keep her safe from everyone.

In the end, I didn't think I had slept more than an hour total. When the sun started rising in the distance, the office was inundated with dim light, and I gave up completely.

I sat up and ran a hand through my hair. Fuck, I probably looked bedraggled, my professor's uniform rumpled, and I hadn't brushed my teeth in a while. Good thing I kept supplies in my office—toothpaste, toothbrush, and a black shirt.

With time to spare before my first class, I took my time getting ready. The jacket of my uniform didn't look good, so I left it behind. I didn't think I'd seen any professor walking around without the full uniform, but there wasn't much I could do about it now.

Thankfully, no one seemed to notice in my first and second morning classes. But as soon as my second class ended and all the students had left, one of Randall's secretaries entered the classroom.

"The headmaster is asking for your presence in his office," she said, sounding like a robot.

"Now?"

She nodded. "Now."

Fuck, what was it this time? Had I been reported for not wearing the suit jacket? That was ridiculous.

But when I entered Randall's office, I realized this was bigger than that.

"Sit," Randall said, his voice flat.

I complied. "You called me?"

Randall nodded. "This morning, I received the visit from two worried parents. Apparently, a professor beat up their son last night."

Was he talking about Tom? "What the fuck?"

"Tom Heyward claims you punched him in the face several times and threatened to kill him."

I gritted my teeth as rage rolled in my veins. "I did threaten him, but I didn't punch him."

"I believe you, but his parents, and now the parents of other students who have heard about the incident, won't. They are asking me to fire you."

My stomach dropped. I couldn't be fired. If I was, then I

wouldn't be able to stay by Erin's side—and I had just learned what could happen if I wasn't there for her.

I clenched my fists. "I didn't punch him. But I did threaten him, and I only did that because he beat up Erin. Actually, he pulled out his Dawnblade and was about to kill her when she was saved." I didn't tell him it hadn't been me. I was already in hot water. No need to pull the others into the pot with me.

"I see." Randall furrowed. "I understand your position, and I also know Tom Heyward is prone to deception, so here's what we're going to do. I'll calm down the parents and I'll let you go with a warning. But don't let something like this happen again. I don't know how long I can protect you."

Protect me. Randall thought he was protecting me. In this situation, maybe. But he had never raised a finger to help me before.

"Is that it?" I asked.

Randall nodded once. "You may go."

I rose from the seat, but didn't move, as another matter itched at my mind. "Why aren't you sending me out to find more members for the half-demon army? Did you give up on that?"

He stared at me, his eyes blank. "I thought you would be busy with your classes this semester. But don't worry about the Black Knight Unit. They are doing fine."

I frowned. I wasn't worried about them. I was concerned why he was so quiet about it. Now that people knew about the army, I thought he would be flashing its members left and right. Or revealing that I was their leader, since I had always been his second.

Not that I wanted to be the Black Knight Unit's leader. I was relieved not to be included in all that anymore. But it brought many more questions to my mind. When he had saved my life and offered me the contract several months ago, I thought he would be using me by now for every little task, no matter how sordid, but he hadn't asked me for anything the last five months.

That was puzzling.

"All right, then," I said, before exiting his office.

I let out a sigh of relief and started for the stairs.

Like a creep, Professor Crimson was waiting for me at the staircase.

"What did he want?" Crimson asked, his voice low.

I considered whether to lie to him, but since he knew about the soul bond and how much Erin meant to me, I didn't think it mattered. So I told him what Tom and his friends had done to Erin, and what I had done to Tom.

"I was dismissed with a warning to not let it happen again," I told him.

"This is perfect," Crimson said, a greedy tone to his voice.

"It is?" I didn't get why.

"Because this shows the parents that Randall doesn't have control over everything that happens at the school," he said. "Parents will be worried that their kids are in here, with so many unstable half-demons on the loose, and they will start doubting Randall's power and influence."

"If you say so," I muttered, eager to get rid of Crimson and the crazed glint in his eyes. He was so consumed by his desire to be the headmaster, he seemed unstable himself.

"Speaking of power," Crimson started. "Randall is the only demon hunter with magic. I could believe he was a half-demon, but his magic isn't dark, or at least it doesn't look like it is. But where does his magic come from? That's your task now, Rey. Find out about Randall's magic. I don't care how. Follow him, break into his office or house after hours, anything. Just figure out where his powers come from."

I wanted to tell him "what if I don't," but I knew what he would say if I tried to rebel. That he would hurt Erin. And she had already been fucking hurt too much for a lifetime.

"Fine," I said through gritted teeth.

7

ERIN

On Saturday night, I waited about an hour after curfew to leave the Gardenia building to meet my mother in the Aster building.

I wore all black, hoping it would help me blend in with the shadows as I crossed the short distance from one building to the other. I was trying to jog and go as fast as I could, even though the bruises on my stomach and chest screamed at me.

It had been two and a half days since the attack, and I could honestly say I was feeling much better, but depending on how I turned or stretched, it still stung like hell.

But what really stung was when I woke up in Rey's bed in the middle of the night and found him nowhere in the house. I thought he was watching over me, making sure I was okay. But no. My friends had taken me to him, probably thinking they were pretty clever, and in the end, all they did was make sure Rey fled and didn't come back to his own house until I was gone.

More indication of that was finding clean clothes neatly

folded outside his bedroom door. It was like there was a note saying "get dressed and get the fuck out of here." It read loud and clear. So, at three in the morning, I hugged my clean clothes—I would wait to change into them after a nice shower in my bathroom—and left his house. Thankfully, I didn't bump into anyone and wasn't harassed.

But I almost had a heart attack when I saw my face in my bedroom mirror. My cheek was dark purple, there was a small scratch on my chin, and my lower lip was split and swollen. My chest and stomach were also purpling from the hits I had taken there.

The next day, I stayed in bed, in an attempt to speed up the healing process. Claire showed up to see me and brought some kind of healing concoction she had found in one of her father's spell books. The thing tasted horrible, but by the end of the day, the bruises were mostly red and quickly disappearing.

My mother had also showed up to see me. She gave me a long lecture about not walking alone, or only with poor Claire, and how I was an easy target, and things like that would keep happening if I gave them opportunity. Of course, we ended up arguing, but she seemed satisfied when I told her I felt good enough to meet her as we first agreed.

I entered the Aster building and went to the top of the south turret, where my mother waited for me. The tower had a big open room at the top, with thin, long windows and a door that led to a small stone balcony. My half-sister, Brianne, had been killed there almost a year ago. Everyone thought it had been a suicide, but those who knew what the mark on her wrist—on my wrist—meant, knew a demon had come for her and killed her.

In the near dark, my mother looked me up and down. "How are you feeling?"

I rolled my shoulders. "Fine. As long as we don't run a mile or spar, I think I'll be fine."

Shaking her head, she turned on a small lantern she had brought with her. The place gained a faint, warm light. "It won't be anything like that."

I walked up to her. "So, what are we doing, then? You mentioned something about magic, if I'm not mistaken."

"Yes. I'm going to teach you some spells I think you'll be able to do because you're ... well, because you're the daughter of the supreme demon."

I crossed my arms. "What are you saying?"

"That you're probably more powerful than any other half-demon at this academy, or anywhere else for that matter, and you should be able to do things no one else can do."

I frowned. "And what is that?"

"I'm going to teach you to syphon power from death," she said, as if it was a normal subject in the academy program, just like demon history or magic spells. "If I'm right, you can take energy from dead bodies and use it to strengthen your magic."

My jaw fell open. "You want me to do what?"

"I know it sounds gruesome, but think about it," she said, her hands moving rapidly. "In a battle, you'll be killing demons. There will be bodies all around you. All you have to do is syphon their residual energy, or life source. That should give your powers a boost."

I shook my head. "That sounds more than gruesome."

"Well, it's a dark spell, so I would say that it's strictly forbidden, but it's a card you can have up your sleeve, just in case." She went to one corner of the room, where there was a big cardboard box. "Here."

She opened the box, and I heard squeaks coming from it.

"What the hell is that?" I approached the box. Several mice ran around the box, trying to get out. I wrinkled my nose. "What are these for?"

"You'll kill them and syphon the energy from them," my mother said.

Staring at her, I took several steps back. "No, I won't."

"What would you rather do? Go after demons? Kill some innocent people? Or perhaps some rabbits?" She pointed to the box. "These are better for practice."

"You're crazy if you think I'm going to do that," I whispered. My stomach twisted at the thought.

"Erin, listen to me." My mother plodded to me. "You need to have an advantage when you fight the demons coming for you. When you fight against your father. This is your advantage. I know it's not ideal, and I know it's nasty, but it'll be useful."

"Even if it is, I can't do it right now. Like you said, in the battlefield, there will be corpses. I can't save those, so maybe, just maybe, I'll be able to do it. But you're talking about killing mice right now."

"What's the big deal? They're just mice."

"That's still killing!" I almost yelled. Since we shouldn't be meeting so late, and talking about something so dark and forbidden, we didn't need unwanted attention.

"Fine, I'll kill them for you."

Without any hesitation, my mother summoned her Dawnblade. She plunged her hand into the box, grabbed a mouse, and then slice her blade across its back.

I turned around as my stomach rolled. Holy shit, I would be sick.

My mother laid five dead mice in front of me. "There. Now do this—"

"Are you serious?" I pressed a hand over my stomach. "I'm about to throw up and you want me to steal the rest of their lifeforce."

"They are already dead," she insisted. "Now all you have to do is take it before it's completely gone. You only have a small window."

Was she this cold and uncaring? It sickened me.

"This is crazy," I whispered, retreating.

"Crazy is the fact that you're hesitating to kill mice. What will happen when demons come for you?" She crossed her arms. "Oh, I know, you'll let them beat you up like you let Tom Heyward."

I clenched my teeth. "I did that because I had no choice. If I handed his ass to him, which I know I could, the other half-demons and I would be in much bigger trouble right now, and you know it!"

"I understand your reasoning, but that doesn't mean I want to see my daughter hurt."

"And I don't want to see this." I gestured to where the mice lay on the stone floor, staining it with their blood.

My mother let out a long sigh. "We could try this with ... I don't know. Cockroaches? But then we would have to kill thousands of them each time you tried the spell. Their energy is too little to be manipulated."

I liked the idea of killing cockroaches much more than killing mice, but I knew it would be hard.

I glanced at the mice and closed my eyes. "I don't want to do this."

"Please, Erin. I'm trying to help you here. You need to be able to do more than cast darkfire and swing a sword if you're going to survive until graduation."

Graduation was less than two years from now.

I frowned. "You think my father will come for me before I graduate?"

"I can't be certain, but I believe so. Honestly, I don't know what is taking him so long. The only thing I know is that he likes games." She shrugged. "Maybe he's taking his time to play with us."

"That is just cruel."

My mother let out a hollow chuckle. "That is who he is. Cruel. Evil. Vicious." She placed a hand on my shoulder. "Please, Erin, just try. The mice are already dead now. Let me run you through it while you try. Okay?"

I didn't like it. Actually, I loathed it. But I understood what my mother was saying. I understood why she was doing it.

Breathing through my mouth, I turned to the mice. "Just for the record, I don't like this."

"It's okay." Standing half a foot behind me, my mother put her hands on my shoulders and pushed me forward. "You don't need to like it. You just need to learn it."

I wrinkled my nose again. Holy shit ... blood covered the mice, staining the stone floor underneath them. If I squinted, the blood mixed with the darkness and I could almost pretend the mice were sleeping instead.

Yeah, that was better. I would think the mice were sleeping.

"I'm ready," I told my mother, even though I didn't feel like it. But if I waited until I felt ready to steal the energy of dead mice, then it would be never.

"All right," my mother started. She went on a long speech

about how I had to channel my magic and use it to guide the energy out of their bodies. I had to use the dark side of my magic and shape it like a giant, invisible hook that I would fish the energy with.

It sounded so simple, but every time I tried to send my magic to the mice, it faded. Not because I couldn't hold on to it, but because I didn't seem to get what I was doing. I lost the nerve before my magic even touched the dead mice, and my power faded.

"I can't do it," I said with an exaggerated sigh.

"You're not trying hard enough!" my mother protested.

I turned to her, my eyes fuming. "I am trying, but I can't. Think about it. I can't do this with mice; you really think that someday I'll be able to do this with demons? Or with people? Even if I know the theory, I won't be able to do it."

"Then you're dead!" my mother shouted. I flinched at her words and the tone of her voice. She let out a long breath. "Sorry. I didn't mean it like that."

"I know what you meant," I muttered.

"Erin, please, try it once more."

I couldn't. Not right now. I shook my head. "I'm done for the night," I whispered before walking away.

I thought my mother would yell at me, curse me, demand I return, but she didn't do any of those things. I was glad she didn't, because I was about to either puke or breakdown, or both, and I didn't want her to see me like that.

What my mother was asking me to do … that was dangerous. Dark. Evil. Not just because I had to use dark magic to perform the spell, but because I was stealing the last energy of dead bodies. It was like stealing their last breaths.

I hated it.

Although this spell might not be for me, I understood

what my mother was trying to do and I tried accepting it—she was looking for an advantage for me. Something I could do that would give me a chance, that would at least buy me more time.

I just wished I didn't have to use dark magic to accomplish it.

8

For about a week, I tried following Randall around, but he was aware of his every move, as if he suspected someone was following him. Even when I shifted into my raven form, he still seemed to hold back.

So that was a bust.

In class, Erin continued the same. In the last week, we had had two other classes, and she acted like the first class. She didn't participate. She didn't even look in my direction, or open her books, or do any of the work I assigned.

She was getting one bad grade after the other, and what upset me was that I knew she was a great student. She was doing it to spite me.

It was fucking working.

To be honest, I thought she would come after me with a vengeance after she spent the night in my bed last week. I knew she was upset that I disappeared and didn't go back all night. I gave her all the space she needed, and hopefully, she slept in before heading to her dorm room.

Our disciplinary action was supposed to be a week ago, exactly on the day she got hurt, but because of that incident, we postponed it.

Her detention was tonight. I was in my classroom in the Hyacinth building, waiting for her, trying—and failing—to grade papers from a quiz I had given earlier in the week.

I probably looked cool and uncaring on the outside, but my heart hammered hard against my chest. In a few minutes, Erin would arrive, and we would be alone in this classroom for ninety minutes.

It would be torture.

It would be fucking paradise.

A knock came from the half-opened door.

I sat straighter. "Come in."

Erin stepped into the classroom. "I'm here." She was dressed in jeans, a black blouse, and flats. Her hair was loose around her shoulders and down her back, and her face was makeup-free. She looked beautiful as always.

I stared at her as a million thoughts crossed my mind.

She looked well, though a little bored. The healing potion I had given her, and the one Claire was putting into her coffee every morning, was helping; there were no more visible bruises on her pretty face.

I was glad she had stood up to Professor Martha about syphoning the life energy of those mice. Yeah, I was a creeper, a stalker, because I had been following her much more closely. After what happened with Tom and his friends, I wouldn't risk it, not even for a few minutes. So, I followed Erin around whenever I could.

Because she had been with her mother that night, I hadn't stayed too close, especially because they would see a suspicious raven flying near the turret, but I had seen enough. Professor Martha was insane if she thought having Erin dig deeper into her dark magic would help her win against King Brikan.

Only a miracle would save Erin against the supreme demon.

And I would either be this fucking miracle or I would come up with one, because Erin would win. It didn't matter how, but Erin would win.

"I see." Letting go of the papers I was grading, I stood. "You can start by polishing the swords we used in class this week." I pointed to the back wall, where a cabinet with the weapons was. "You'll find a rag, the polish, and everything you need in the cabinet."

She frowned. "That is all? Polish the swords?"

"For now, yes."

She nodded once, then retreated to the back wall.

And I had to force myself to sit down and resume grading my papers. Though, I had to admit, I would grade everything wrong. So I pushed the papers aside but tried to plan my lessons for next week. Even if I listed topics, at least I was doing something useful.

My eyes shifted to the stack of papers I had been grading. Right on top was Erin's quiz. She hadn't answered one question. It wasn't that she hadn't answered them right. She hadn't even written her entire name on it. Just "E."

I stared at her across the room. She pulled the swords from the cabinet and spread them over the sparring mat. Then, with the rag and polish in hand, she sat down in the middle of the swords. She reached for the closest one, placed it on top of her folded legs, and began polishing it.

Looking at her right now was like looking at her in class —she was there, but her mind wasn't. She didn't pay attention to a word I said, or to whatever she was supposed to do. There was a permanent dull light in her eyes, as if it was too painful for her to do anything else other than mope.

Than mourn.

I hated seeing her like this.

She was so absentminded, when she changed swords, one slipped and fell to her side with a faint clank.

Erin gasped and clutched at her index finger.

"What is it?" I asked, already halfway to her. I hopped over the swords on the floor and knelt beside her. "What happened?"

"Nothing," she said, not looking at me. She still held on to her finger.

"Let me see." I grabbed her hands and pulled them toward me. A red line stained the tip of Erin's index finger. "You cut yourself."

"It's nothing." She tugged on her hands.

I tsked, not in the mood to argue. Instead, I shot up, went back to my desk on the other corner of the room, opened a drawer, and got gauze, an antibiotic cream, and a Band-Aid from the first aid kit. When I went back to her, Erin finally looked at me, her golden eyes huge. Wary.

I sat down beside her. "It'll be okay," I said, taking her hand and placing it in my lap. I cleaned the cut with the gauze, wiping most of the blood away. The cut was small but in a sensitive spot. It began bleeding again right away.

I pressed the gauze to the cut, hoping to stop the bleeding with the pressure.

"You don't need to do this," Erin said, tugging her hand back.

I held on to her wrist. "Some of these swords are old and rusty. We should make sure this cut won't give you trouble later."

"Then I can do it myself."

I stared at her. "Erin, I want to do this."

She swallowed hard.

"I'm sorry," she said in a whisper.

I frowned. "For?"

"For my friends taking me to your house that day. If I had known they were taking me to your house, or if I had been more conscious about what was happening, I wouldn't have let them. I would have rather taken my chances in the infirmary."

"You're so averse to me that besides spacing out during my classes, you would have rather been mistreated and injured more, or worse?"

Her eyes hardened. "*I'm* averse to *you*? Are you for real?"

"Then what is it?"

"You're the one who wants nothing to do with me! I was dumped at your house, and then you disappeared because you couldn't stand having me there."

My jaw went slack. She thought I had disappeared because I disliked her? Was she crazy? "I won't answer that," I muttered. It was killing me to let her think that, but if it meant she would keep her distance from me, then so be it.

"When I woke up in the middle of the night and saw my clothes beside the door, I left," she said. "I wish I had a way of letting you know. Oh, hey, I just left your house. You can come back now."

"You left? In the middle of the night?" I asked, my gut tensing. "What time was that?"

She shrugged. "I don't remember exactly. Maybe three in the morning?"

Holy fuck, she had been walking alone around campus at three in the morning, while I was trying to nap in my office. What if something had happened to her?

One more reason I should never take my eyes off her.

Something vicious swam in my veins, and I clenched my teeth hard to contain it inside of me. I wasn't mad at her. I was mad at this fucking situation.

I took a deep, calming breath. "Erin, you can't go around alone, okay? Especially not in the middle of the night."

Her brows curled down. "Should I hire a babysitter twenty-four-seven?"

"That wouldn't be a bad idea," I snapped. She couldn't talk seriously about this? She had to answer like that? She pulled her hand from mine. "Stop being so stubborn and let me see it." I grabbed her hand and pulled off the gauze. The bleeding had stopped.

Gently, I applied the cream over the cut, then wrapped a Band-Aid around it.

A force stronger than myself and my will hit me hard. I placed a kiss on top of the Band-Aid. Erin went still. Before I could stop myself, I turned her hand, leaned closer, and kissed the inside of her wrist. Erin inhaled sharply.

I locked my eyes on hers, and something there pulled me in. I couldn't stop myself even if I wanted to.

And I sure didn't want to.

Pulling her to me, I leaned over her. Erin didn't resist. In fact, when I lowered my mouth to hers, she answered right away. I brushed my lips over hers and she let out a long sigh, as if she had been waiting for that. She parted her lips for me, letting me in.

My mouth glued to hers, I snaked my arm around her waist and laid her down on the mat, careful with all the swords around us, and pressed my body to hers. Her taste was sweet on my tongue, and her enticing rose scent filled my nostrils, and intoxicated my mind.

Erin wound her legs around my hips, locking me close to her. She snaked her hands around my shoulders and buried her nails in my back. Even through my clothes, I could feel how sharp and long they were. This kind of pain was pleasure.

Slowly, I slipped my hand under her blouse, feeling the warm and silky skin of her stomach, the hard planes of the muscles underneath. My hand went up and up, until my fingertips teased the outline of her bra.

Gasping against my mouth, Erin arched her back into my touch. Unable to resist, I pressed my hips into hers. Could she feel how much I wanted her? How much I craved her?

This ... this was heaven. I could die right now and I would die satisfied.

Erin's hands traveled south, around my middle, down my hips. She grabbed the waist of my pants, her fingertips sneaking underneath as she undid the button.

I stilled.

Wait.

This was heaven, but I didn't deserve heaven.

Breaking the kiss, I jumped up and moved several feet from her. "This isn't right," I muttered.

Erin propped herself on her elbows, her eyes round. "Are you serious?"

I shook my head, trying to clear the fog from my mind. While she stayed here, the risk of losing control was too great. "You should go."

Cheeks reddening, Erin unfolded from the floor. "I don't understand ..."

"There's nothing to understand." I averted my gaze, lest the disappointed and frustrated glint in her eyes make me regret this decision. "I'm your professor; you're a student. This is not just wrong, it's forbidden." If she didn't hear any other of my reasons to stay away, she had to hear that. Because if we were caught, I would be fired, and if I was fired, I couldn't protect her. "This disciplinary action is done. Over. You can go now."

For a moment, Erin didn't move at all. I thought I would have to say something terrible to her so she would finally run from me, but it wasn't necessary. When she marched away from the classroom, I got a glimpse of her face. Besides her disappointment, her eyes also told me she was mortified.

Holy fuck.

I needed a breather. I needed some time far away from her, to calm my mind and body, before I broke down and told her exactly how I felt.

But I couldn't get away from her.

Like the fucking creep I was, I sucked it up and went after her. Outside the Hyacinth building, I shifted into my raven and followed her as she ran to the Gardenia building.

Hadn't I told her to not walk alone around campus? Especially at night?

That was why I was following her. After what happened with Tom, I didn't feel right leaving her alone for a minute. Though I needed distance from her, I couldn't abandon her. I would rather suffer through my agony, my desire, my pain, than risk having her hurt again.

I perched on the branches of a tree beside the building

and watched as Erin ran through the front door, wiping at her face. Fuck, she was crying.

I felt like a giant jerk.

I stayed on the tree branch until the lights of her room came on. Then I flew away. I would fly around for a few minutes, hoping the cool air of the night sky calmed my racing heart and brought reason to my mind.

9

ERIN

WORSE THAN BEING PUSHED AWAY after being kissed by Rey? Having to go to his class. I ignored him and his lectures and lessons even more.

During the first half of class, I kept my book closed and my eyes out the window, trying hard to shut all of his words out. During the second half, I sat down on a corner of the mat —the same one we had tangled together on—and pretended nothing was going on.

One day, Claire sat down beside me for a moment. "Everyone is noticing something is wrong," she told me. Of course, she knew what had happened between Rey and me.

That night, I had run back to my dorm with tears burning my eyes. Once I was inside my bedroom, I let myself cry for two minutes. Then I was done. Until the next day when Claire asked me how the disciplinary action went and I started crying again.

I had felt dirty and ashamed. If I let the dark thoughts in my mind do the talking, I would believe Rey was toying with me.

Kissing me here and there, then kicking me out like a stray dog. And every time I remembered he had pulled back right when I reached for his pants, my cheeks warmed with embarrassment. What? He thought all that kissing wasn't going anywhere? My body screamed for his every moment of the day. I wasn't sure if it was part of the soul bond, but I was tired of it. And now Rey probably thought I was a whore, reaching for his pants like that.

If only I could bury myself in a hole and never come out again.

Pretending to be cool about it all, I looked around the classroom. The students kept stealing glances at me and whispering.

"That's nothing new," I said in a low voice. "They do that all the time, mostly because I'm my father's daughter."

"But they are starting to notice you act like this only in Rey's class," Claire said. "Maybe you should try to act normal in his classes, Erin. That will be less suspicious."

I shook my head. "I can't. You know I can't."

Despite myself, my traitorous eyes found him across the classroom. He was like a magnet. Even when I didn't want to look at him, I always found him as if he was a beacon calling for me.

Only I didn't call to him. I repelled him.

He was demonstrating a move to two students, looking so elegant and powerful in his uniform. Every time I saw him fighting, he looked like a martial artist, with the precise moves, the right strength, the perfect finish.

He was freaking perfect.

Except for when he was a jerk and pushed me away.

Seriously, how long would it take for me to learn he would always be like that? I shouldn't give him openings to use and play with me like that night. I shouldn't have hope that this would become something more.

I was foolish.

When class was dismissed, I was the first one out the door. I waited for Claire outside, and then we walked from the Hyacinth building to the cafeteria on the first floor of the dorms.

On the way, we witnessed other students picking on half-demons. Since they joined our classes as students a week ago, the full-blood demon hunters had been meaner and the protests from the parents had continued. Twice, I had been surrounded and yelled at, but thankfully, I hadn't been alone. For some reason, Harvey, Ava, Harper, and even Peter seemed to always be a hop away. Whenever they saw something suspicious, they came and helped Claire and me.

Things weren't any different in the cafeteria. The half-demons were shoved and threatened in the lunch line, and harassed while they were eating quietly. Though most of them—us—tried to stay quiet, some of the half-demons had hot tempers. They responded, turning the situation into a fight and ending up in Randall's office.

Whenever that happened, whispers spread like wildfire.

"Did you see it? I told you they're unstable."

"They aren't just unstable. They are also evil."

"It's just a matter of time before they attack and kill us all."

I confess, even I had trouble holding back. I wanted to summon my darkfire and release it on them all. I wouldn't hit to kill, but damn, I wished I could throw my magic at them, enough to inflict a little pain.

Without any complications, Claire and I made it through

the lunch line, and we went to our usual table along the glass wall.

I sat down, but she put her tray on the table and said, "I need to go to the restroom. Be right back."

I watched as she weaved through the tables and disappeared down the hallway that led to the restrooms.

A moment later, a new tray appeared beside mine.

"Hi," Harper said, taking a seat beside me.

"Hey, girl." I smiled at her, glad to not be alone. I was never a wimp, but it would be foolish of me to pretend I wasn't wary of being among so many ill-meaning students. "How is it going?"

Harper shrugged. "I've been better."

"What do you mean?"

"Claire hasn't paid much attention to me," she said, her tone dejected. "I mean, as a friend or a classmate. But no more than that."

I frowned. "Hm, Harper, I think that might be because of two things. One, I'm not sure Claire realizes you're into her. To her, you're a good friend. You know what I mean?" Claire would only figure out that Harper liked her if Harper made it clear. "And two—"

"She still hasn't forgotten Tanner," Harper finished for me.

"It's not that she can't forget him; it's that it was an intense and damaging relationship," I explained. "It'll take some time for her to recover from that."

"I know, I know." She sighed. "I guess I just have to be here and be a good *friend* to her until she's ready."

"Hang in there," I told her. "If I have my way, you two will get together someday."

Harper smiled at me.

"Who will get together with whom?" Claire asked, sitting down by my side.

"In the movie," Harper said quickly.

"Movie?" Claire asked. She grabbed her utensils and started picking at her food. "What movie?"

"Tonight," Harper said. "I heard there will be a romantic suspense movie playing in the movie room tonight."

"Do you know where it is located?" I asked, curious. Each semester, the movie room moved. Sometimes, if there was danger of the movie room being found, it moved in the middle of the semester.

"I do." Harper nodded. "I was told it was a good movie to bring a date to." I shook my head at Harper. What the hell was she doing? Claire wasn't ready. She went on, "What about you, Claire? Don't you want to bring a date to the movie tonight?"

Claire's shoulders sagged. "No movies or dates for me." She pierced her forked through the french fries, as if she could hurt them. "My heart can't handle anything like that right now."

"I see," Harper muttered, her tone sad.

Shit, I knew it. Why did she poke around so soon? Now Claire had been reminded of Tanner, and Harper was sad because she still had no chance here.

We finished eating in silence, each of us lost in her own head. And, I would bet, all of us thinking about our doomed love lives. Claire was sighing over Tanner, Harper was daydreaming about Claire, and I was crying over Rey.

Now we just needed to be joined by Ava, who was always after Harvey, and we would have a full party of heartbroken girls. Maybe we should form a band. What would be a cool name for us? The Leftovers, or the Ones Left Behind, or the Forgotten, or the Unwanted.

I snickered.

Claire glanced at me. "What is it?"

"Nothing," I muttered.

A moment later, Professor Graham entered the cafeteria. "All students proceed to the courtyard. Headmaster Randall has an announcement."

Most students rushed out, but Claire, Harper, and I took our time getting up from our table, putting the trays away, and walking to the courtyard.

"Is there another ball coming up that I don't know about?" I asked as we halted behind the throng of students, professors, and other staff milling around the courtyard, everyone facing the back of the Aster building. "Or maybe an event?"

"Not that I remember," Claire said, sounding as curious as I was.

Soon, the headmaster walked out the Aster building. He smiled, like a rock star greeting his fans. In a way, I guess he was a rock star in our world. Even more than the full-fledged demon hunters, since he was the first one, the founder of the Blackthorn Hunters and the academy. And though people seemed smitten by him, they didn't go crazy like they had done with the demon hunters last semester.

"I'm here to announce I made a deal with the protestors and the school board," he said, his voice loud and clear, as if he spoke into a microphone. Whatever chatter or whispers had been running through the crowd ceased. "A contest will be held at the end of the next semester. This contest, called the Shadow Trials, will help us determined which of the half-demon students are worthy of continuing at the academy."

The chatter and whispers came back, fueled by outrage and lots of questions.

The headmaster continued, "Anyone who passes the Shadow Trials will be fully accepted by the demon hunters here. Anyone who doesn't will be cast out—if they don't die first, because this will be a deadly contest."

I shook my head, not believing what I was hearing.

"Is he serious?" Claire asked me in a whisper.

I wished I could tell her he wasn't.

"The half-demons will be given a year to study here," the headmaster continued, "to learn as much as they can before the contest. Meanwhile, the half-demons will be treated with respect and equality. If they aren't, I'll punish those who disobey me." He waved his hands, dismissing us. "Now everyone go back to your classes."

Just like that, the headmaster walked into the Aster building, leaving all of us speechless but full of questions.

People dispersed, but all of them were talking about this contest.

"He just drops a bomb like that, then leaves us to ponder," Harper said, taking the words right out of my mouth.

"There's nothing we can do about it," Claire said. "Besides, this contest is at the end of next semester. Anything can happen before then."

"That's true," I muttered, though I wasn't satisfied with the lack of information.

"Let's go to class," Claire said.

We started walking to the Statice building.

"Erin."

I whipped in the direction of her voice. My mother walked toward me, her steps fast. From the set of her mouth and the hard line of her brows, I knew she was upset.

"What is it?" I asked.

She halted in front of me. "You're a half-demon. Everyone knows that."

"Oh-kay. And?"

She pressed her lips tight before blurting, "You'll have to participate in the Shadow Trials."

I WATCHED the whole announcement from the corner of the Orchid building. What the fuck was Randall playing at? A deadly contest for the half-demons? This had to be some kind of sick joke.

Randall delivered the half-baked speech and left without any explanation. The students started going to their classes, all talking about the Shadow Trials. Erin also turned and walked away until her mother stopped her. From this far, I couldn't hear what they were talking about, but judging by the way all the blood drained from Erin's face, it couldn't be good.

Was Martha proposing more crazy experiments and spells? Hadn't she realized Erin wasn't up for dark magic like that?

The two of them resumed walking, soon leaving my line of sight.

At least I knew Erin would be okay for the next few minutes. Meanwhile, I could do something else. I went into the Aster building and knocked on Randall's office.

"Come in," he said.

I walked in and closed the door behind me. "What's going on?"

Randall stood behind his desk, watching the window and all the students leaving the courtyard. He glanced at me. "What do you mean?"

"This fucking contest. The Shadow Trials. What is that all about?"

He didn't answer at first, making me think he wouldn't. What? Now I wasn't his dear second anymore, and he was keeping more stuff from me? Not that I fucking cared, but this … this was important.

Finally, he said, "I had to appease the protestors and even the professors who are strictly against teaching the half-demons. That was the only solution I could think of."

"I bet you could have come up with something better."

"Believe me, I've tried, but nothing seemed good enough for them."

I shook my head. "I can't believe that. A deadly contest? It doesn't seem right."

"At least it'll be entertaining." He sat down at his desk. "A few lives will be lost, but those survive will be able to stay without discrimination."

"Do you really believe the discrimination will stop after that?"

Randall sucked in a sharp breath. "I guess we'll have to wait and see."

"I know you can stop this if you want."

"I won't because, when it's time, I'll assign the Shadow Trials to the full-fledged demon hunters. They will take care of it."

"But—"

"Rey, this contest is happening; there's no way around it." He leaned forward on the desk, his dark eyes dull. "And I should inform you: You're a half-demon. You'll also take part in the Shadow Trials."

What the ... "Only a handful of people know I'm a half-demon."

"I know, but that will change closer to the contest."

I took a step forward. "Are you threatening me?"

Randall let out a hollow chuckle. "You might be old and powerful, Reyan, but I'm older and more powerful. I don't need to threaten you. If I wanted, I could squash you with my thoughts." He waved me off. "Now get out of my sight. I have much to do."

I clenched my teeth, my jaw hurting from the pressure. The rage whipping around me demanded I lunge over the desk and punch him, but Randall was fucking right. He was much more powerful than I was. I would never be able to touch him if he didn't want me to.

I strutted out of his office before I did something stupid.

In need of some release, I climbed up the stairs until I was on the top floor, at a balcony that opened up in the middle of the roof. It wasn't as high as the turrets at the corners of the building, but it would do. After taking a good look around, I shifted into my raven and flew up.

I hadn't shifted so much in months, maybe even years, but lately it seemed it was all I could do to clear my head and calm my breathing. High in the sky, I flew around the perimeter of the academy.

But instead of clearing my mind, many thoughts knotted together.

What was Randall's point with the Shadow Trials? What

did he want with it? And what was that about revealing who I was and putting me in the contest?

Did that mean he planned on having Erin participate in the contest too?

Erin ...

She had been even worse in class since that disciplinary-action-gone-wrong. Completely absentminded and always looking sad. It broke my fucking heart.

If only she knew how much restraint it had taken to stop myself that night, if only she knew how I was trying to keep her safe, if only she understood my side of things.

If only she knew I was trying to do the honorable thing and respect her mother's wishes—threats.

Even if I sat down with her and explained it detail by detail, I didn't think she would agree with me. That was why I didn't tell her, why I didn't ask her if it was okay.

For now, I avoided her as much as I could, while sticking to the shadows to make sure she was safe.

Since I didn't have any classes that afternoon, I flew around the academy, eventually checking on Erin whenever I knew she would be out of the buildings to either switch classes, or to go to the cafeteria.

Or to go to her dorm.

I perched atop the Gardenia building and watched as she walked in with Claire and Harper for the evening. If she kept to her habits, she would have dinner with her friends in the cafeteria, then they would get together for a little while in one of their bedrooms, and later they would turn in for the night.

I took flight when I saw them entering Claire's room, sure that they wouldn't leave for another hour, and went to stretch my wings some more. The full moon was high in the sky, almost obscuring the many stars dotting the darkness. It was a beautiful, warm night, and I wished the rest of the world was as peaceful as the night sky.

I lost track of time. It was probably almost midnight when I rounded the outer walls of the academy, attempting to go back to my townhouse, and spotted something that caught my attention.

A shadow moving fast through the trees.

Faster than the shadow, I flew down, but kept my distance, in case it was some demon. Honestly, the first thing that came to mind was that this was a demon doing a reconnaissance mission for King Brikan.

But it wasn't that.

The shadowy figure was a man in a heavy black cloak, its hood covering most of his face.

Wanting a better look, I flew ahead of the figure and paused on a low branch. The man walked past me and I almost yelped in surprise.

Randall.

What the fuck was he doing out this late at night?

I couldn't waste this opportunity, so I followed Randall, careful not to catch his attention. I didn't think he knew I could shapeshift into a raven, but I wouldn't risk that now.

I didn't have to follow him long. Randall halted in front of an arched tree. He raised his hands high and chanted something in a muted voice. Dark light shone from the arched tree trunk, creating a thin black wall that touched the ground.

A portal.

Without hesitation, Randall entered the portal.

I flew forward, but stopped myself. Who knew where this fucking portal was going? It could very well go to the underworld for all I knew, a place I was not welcome. If I went into the underworld, I wasn't coming back alive.

I knew Randall had to come back sometime, so I perched on a high branch near the portal and waited.

Waiting ... not my strong suit.

I almost caved and entered the portal several times. I was glad I didn't, because almost an hour later, Randall walked out.

His hood was down, showing off all the blood staining his chin and neck. My stomach knotted. There was blood on his hands too.

Was ... had he drank blood? From whom?

Where the fuck did that portal lead?

The portal faded behind him. Randall pulled up the hood of his cloak and dashed away in the direction of the academy, just as fast as he had come earlier.

Despite wanting to be far away from him, I followed just to make sure he wasn't going to stop anywhere else, open up another portal, and repeat whatever shit he had done.

But he didn't. He went directly to the academy.

For a moment, I wondered how he would get past the guards without anyone seeing the blood all over him, but I should have known better. Randall used his magic to have the guards walk away from one of the outposts. He casually walked through the small gate and strolled to the Aster building—unseen.

I swooped over the academy one more time before retreating for the night, my mind reeling with what I had seen. What the hell had I witnessed? Why was Randall covered in blood?

There was only one way to find out.

I would have to follow Randall again.

ERIN

I HADN'T SLEPT WELL since my mother told me I would have to participate in the Shadow Trials next semester, and that was over a week ago. Well, not that I ever slept well, but it was even worse than before.

And the freaking nightmares didn't stop. More than before, I saw Brianne and Cindy in my dreams, asking me to help them, to save them, to come with them. Once or twice, I thought they were trying to tell me more, but since I couldn't walk to them, they couldn't utter the right words. And the dream still ended the same way.

During our third meeting, my mother noticed I was having problems focusing.

"What's wrong?" she asked, standing right beside the dead mice as if it were as normal as standing in front of the whiteboard in her classroom.

I let out a long sigh. No reason not to tell her now. "I can't sleep well because I keep having nightmares about Brianne and Cindy." I went on and explained the nightmares to her: Brianne and Cindy showed up in normal places, but they always looked like zombies. They begged me to help them, but I couldn't move a muscle. Demons came for them, and there was nothing I could do. "I always wake up when the demons turn to me."

My mother frowned. "This nightmare ... it might have a meaning."

"What do you mean?"

"Maybe they are trying to tell you something. You should try asking them."

"They can't seem to say anything other than to ask for help."

"The dream is yours," my mother said. "You should be able to manipulate it a little."

"Easier said than done," I muttered.

"Speaking of telling something ..."

My back straightened. This couldn't be good. "What?"

"It occurred to me that you might not know that King Brikan has more children out there," she said, as if it was a big confession.

"Well, he had Brianne, Cindy, and me." And Tanner. But I didn't tell her that. Not yet. "Are there more?"

My mother nodded. "Many more. I ... I found out King Brikan was always very busy taking the form of a human man and seducing women. As far as I know, he wanted to create as many children as he could."

My stomach tightened. If I felt a little nauseous about it, I couldn't imagine what my mother thought. What she felt. But this was an opportunity. Brianne and Cindy were gone, and Tanner was a guy, which meant I was alone to fulfill a prophecy that said three of his daughters would step up and take his kingdom.

"How can I find them?" I asked.

My mother's eyes rounded and she recoiled as if I had slapped her. "What? Why would you want to find them?"

"Because!" I let out another long sigh, not really sure about this, but the time for lies was over. "I found a legend, sort of like a prophecy. It's called the Demon Kissed Queens, and—"

"I know what you're getting at," my mother said, interrupting me. She raised her index finger. "I know you think you're one of these queens and you need to find the other two, so you three can defeat the supreme demon, but let me tell you, it won't work like that. He is too damn powerful to be stopped by an old legend like that."

"How can you be so sure?" I gestured to the dead mice behind her. "Why not believe that, when you believe I can syphon the energy of dead bodies to help defend myself against him?"

"Because this spell is a last resort, your last line of defense so you can *run* from him," she barked at me. "I'm not going to help you march toward him, Erin. In fact, sometimes I think we should pack and run."

I gasped. "Run?"

"Yes. Think about it. He knows you're here. And as I keep saying, it's only a matter of time until he shows up. If we run, we can hide. He won't know where you are. If we keep running, if we are careful and don't stop, he won't find you."

I shook my head. "I've already moved too many times in my life, and even then, I had stopped for a while. Run until the day I die? No, I won't do that. I'm not a coward."

My mother groaned. "Erin, just think about it. There's no way to locate them. How you're going to do it? Go around the academy asking if someone else is the daughter or son of King Brikan? Or maybe around Chasseur Ville? It'll be impossible to find them. And let's say you did find them, do you think all of them know who they are, what they can do? Do you think they will want to join you and fight against the most powerful being in existence?" I averted my eyes. Damn it, she had a point. A long breath escaped her lips. "You should focus on things we can control, like practicing spells that will make you more powerful."

"Like killing innocent animals and syphoning their energy?" I asked, the sarcasm clear in my voice.

Ignoring my tone, my mother pointed to the dead mice again. "Yes. Now focus and try again."

I rolled my shoulders. I wanted to argue more, but I knew she had a good point. Searching for my half-siblings was an impossible task, and convincing them to join me would be even worse.

I archived that in the back of my mind—I would think more about what I could do with this information later—and turned to the dead mice. I might not like this, but I understood why I had to do it.

Though, I hadn't been able to kill the mice yet. Once more, my mother had sliced through them and placed them on the ground for me. Right on top of the bloodstain from the previous two times we had practiced.

Inhaling deeply, I channeled my magic. I imagined I had a knitting needle and I used it to find the corners of dark magic hidden in my veins, tugging at them, pulling them to me, knitting them together to create something more, something I could control, something I could use.

When I felt a heavy mesh of dark magic swirling inside me, I sent it out toward the mice. My magic enveloped them like a net, seeking the little energy they still had within. I felt it when my magic found it, a tiny ball of life. Not sure what I was doing, I raised my arm in front of myself and hooked the air. My magic dipped in and hooked the energy.

I closed my hand and pulled it like a rope.

The magic tugged at the energy.

The damn energy was more stubborn than I thought.

I sent more dark magic to the dead mice. I swirled it around them.

Around us.

Around the tower.

The dark magic filled me up, giving me strength, making me powerful. At that moment, I was sure I could do anything. I could face Brikan and win. I could even face Randall at the same time.

There was so much power thrumming inside my veins. A shift in the magic jolted over me. It took over my muscles and my lungs. I felt I was drowning in a black river.

"Erin!"

I released the magic, and it ricocheted like an elastic string. I fell on my knees, gasping for air.

My mother reached for me, holding my shoulders up. "Are you okay?"

I nodded. A little out of breath, and a little shaken by what I had just done, but otherwise okay. "Yes." I coughed, then inhaled deeply, trying to calm my racing heart. "I'm sorry. I lost control of my magic."

"Dark magic," she whispered. "I know. It's harder to control. It's like it has a life of its own. I've heard that before." She held on to my hands and helped me up. "You just have to keep practicing. That's the only way to get better at this."

I stared at her. "You want me to keep doing this? Didn't you just see what I did? I could have killed you."

"But you didn't. You stopped before you could harm me."

She patted my hand. "I believe in you, and I know you can control your dark magic."

I pulled my hand away from her. "I don't want to do this anymore."

She nodded. "I understand. Then we can try something else."

Didn't she hear me? "Something else?"

"Yes." She stood beside the dead mice again. "Instead of syphoning their energy, you can do something like necromancy and reanimate them."

"W-what?"

"Imagine on the battlefield, lots of bodies around you. If you can't syphon their life source and become stronger that way, you can reanimate them and have an army to fight alongside you."

I blinked, sure she didn't hear herself. "That is insane. I won't reanimate dead bodies!"

My mother's face turned into a scowl. "Don't you get it? You have to be able to do things no one else can in order to survive."

"I won't compromise my morals in order to save my life! I would rather die than have a dead army beside me."

My mother advanced a step, and for a moment, I thought she would hit me. She halted and clenched her hands. Her knuckles turned white. "I'm done with you tonight. Just go."

"Gladly," I said, before scurrying out the turret.

Did she really think I liked this? Stealing lifeforce and bringing back the dead? That was straight out of a horror movie. *So* not me.

Besides, messing with dark magic like that? I didn't like it. I felt like someday I would lose control over it and I would hurt her, my friends, hurt myself. And I really didn't want to hurt anyone.

Once out the Aster building, I paused.

Speaking of hurting ... ever since the incident with Tom, I had been very wary of walking around campus, even when I was with Claire and Harper. But right now? It was freaking late. The campus was dark and eerie, and I was alone.

I didn't like it.

I shook my head once and ran from the back of the Aster building to the Gardenia building. At least they weren't too far apart, and running made feel like I could escape if someone came after me.

I didn't even want to take the time to appreciate the beautiful and warm night sky, and the waning moon, and the stars. Soon enough, it would be too cold to enjoy nights like this. Not that I could enjoy them right now. It was just freaking dangerous for me, no matter where I went.

I slowed down when I arrived at the front door of the Gardenia building. A shadow cut over me. My heart stopped and I looked up. A raven flew by and perched atop a tree at the corner of the building.

"Shit," I muttered, letting out a long breath. The freaking bird had scared me to death.

But after the first scare, I looked at the bird. The raven was a silhouette in the dark, but I couldn't stop thinking it looked pretty. I envied this raven. It was free to fly anywhere it wanted to. It could go far away, not afraid of anything.

Unlike me.

Shaking my head, I entered the building and went to my bedroom.

It was almost midnight, but two seconds after I closed my door, a knock echoed.

Knowing who it was, I opened the door again. "Hey, you."

Claire held up two steaming mugs and smiled at me. "I come bearing gifts."

I ushered her in and locked the door behind her.

She handed me one of the mugs, filled to the brim with tea, and sat down on my bed. "So, how was practice tonight?"

I wrinkled my nose and sat down beside her. "Ugh, my mother now doesn't just want me to kill mice and steal their energy, but she also wants me to try to reanimate them."

Claire's head jerked back. "What? That's hardcore dark magic!"

"I know," I said with a sigh. "As usual, we argued more than practiced." I sipped from my tea. "But I found out something interesting."

Claire blew on her mug, cooling her tea. "What?"

"Apparently, King Brikan has many children, which means I could find them. I could get them together and we could fight him. We could win." Never mind the fact that some could not want to join me. This was wishful thinking more than anything.

"That's a great idea, but ..." Claire pursed her lips before continuing, "It would be too hard to accomplish."

"Yeah, my mother already mentioned that. Some of these children could be old or really young. Some of them won't know what they are or whose children they are. And most won't want to join me. Don't worry, my mother already lectured me about that."

"Not only that, but to go after them, you would have to leave the academy," Claire said. "And you know you're safer here. If you leave, you'll be in terrible danger."

I snorted. "Safer here? You did hear the announcement about the Shadow Trials, didn't you? That's a deadly contest.

You know I'll have to take part in that." I tried not thinking about that too much, because it only added stress to my already huge list of problems.

"Well, we still have to figure something out for that."

I raised an eyebrow. "Are you planning on stopping an entire contest? Or maybe hide me away so I don't have to take part?"

She chuckled. "Maybe. I don't know. I'm just saying. We have done some pretty amazing things in the last year. I bet we can do some more." She winked.

I shook my head. "If I didn't know you and how easily scared you get, I would say you love getting into the kind of messes we often find ourselves in."

"Sometimes I do; sometimes I don't."

I laughed at that, amused that when it was only the two of us, Claire put on a bravado she didn't usually have. She could be a scaredy-cat, but she always stayed by my side, and even when our chances were lower than zero, she sucked it up and helped me in way only she could.

And I loved her for that.

Though I thought Claire and my mother were partially right about my half-siblings, I didn't want to give up hope yet. Finding them might be near impossible, but I wanted to find a way.

I had to.

For days, I tried following Randall, but he didn't go back to the forest, at least not when I was nearby.

Giving up on that plan for now, I headed to the library late one Friday night, to see if I could find any clues about whatever the fuck Randall had done inside that portal. Of course, I had peeked in on Erin before coming to the library. I had to make sure she was in her dorm and not walking around campus by herself. At least tonight, she didn't seem to have one of those gruesome practices with her mother.

What was Professor Martha thinking? Dark magic? Reanimating corpses? I was glad Erin stuck to her morals and refused to do any of that. If she went down that rabbit hole, the dark magic would only grow stronger and one day consume her.

We already had a lot of trouble on our hands as it was.

After confirming Erin was indeed in her room, I went to the library. It was closed and dark, but nothing a little magic couldn't fix. I unlocked the door and navigated through the main part of the library in the dark, but when I reached the restricted section, I conjured a small darkfire ball. It floated above the room, illuminating much less than the lights on the ceiling, but enough so I wouldn't get caught.

Not that I would get in trouble for being here, regardless of the time of the day, but I really didn't want anyone to know what I was about to research.

I started pulling out books on curses and dark rituals.

Hours and dozens of books later, I had found nothing about a curse or ritual that involved a portal and blood, at least not ones with the descriptions that fit the scene I witnessed.

Where else could I find books about such topics? Professor Crimson was known for having an extensive library of dark magic books in his townhouse, but I was sure he was there right now. Breaking in would be too hard.

Then, there was Randall's private collection. Adjacent to his office, there was an extensive room with thousands of books of all kinds. I had only entered that library once or twice, while Randall was talking to me about other things. I remembered being impressed by the few collections I had seen there.

I glanced at my phone. It was past ten at night. Randall stayed in his office until after midnight most nights. I could either wait until the middle of the night, or I could go and check now.

Deciding it was best to check now, just in case, I exited the Iris building and shifted into my raven. I flew across the courtyard, swirling around the blackthorn tree, to the Aster building.

From a distance, I saw the window to his office was dark, but when I flew by, I confirmed the room was empty.

I nosedived, and in the shadows of the building, I shifted

into my human form. I entered the building and raced to Randall's private library. For a moment, I wondered if my magic would work on this door, but when I tried, the door unlocked right away. I guess Randall didn't think he had to worry about other magical users at the academy, except for me. Well, that had been true until a few months ago when he brought the half-demons to the school. Most half-demons had magic.

I shook my head. That didn't matter. All that mattered was that I was now inside his library, and I had a book to find. Randall's private library had no windows, but even then I only cast a darkfire ball and sent it floating through the room, lest the glow of the normal lights shine from under the door and someone who might be walking by saw it.

I glanced around. Rows and rows with little space between them, crammed with all kinds of books—hastily bounds books, leather ledgers, binders, and even a few rolled parchments.

How would I ever find a book about what I was looking for here, when I didn't even know what that was exactly?

I walked among the shelves, reading the spines and trying to get the gist of the kinds of books in here.

Demonology 101
The Darkest Spells
The Worst Demons to Encounter and How to Stop Them
Demonic Contracts
All About Witches Volume One
All About Witches Volume Two
All About Witches Volume Three

And more books about supernaturals, dark magic, and everything about demons and demonology.

Among so many fucking books, wasn't there anything about curses and rituals?

I weaved among shelves, until I noticed that what I believed was the back of the room was only the first half of it. The wall extended to almost the entire width of the library, but in the farthest corner was a small archway. I glanced back. It was impossible to see the archway from the door because of the shelves blocking it.

Wary, I stepped through the archway into a wide room lined with glass shelves containing all sorts of weird objects. Amulets, scepters, bowls, feathers, and small vials with colorful liquids—were those potions?

But what caught my attention was the bronze pedestal in the middle of the room and the thick, open book on top of it.

Holding my breath, I walked to the book. The open page was about a ritual to steal powers from a witch. What the ...

Rituals. This book was about rituals.

I flipped through the book some more, but realized some of the pages were marked. I flipped to the first marker. The text on that page described a ritual to exorcise demons from humans, like Randall had done with Tanner and Orzon last semester. The next marker was a ritual to detect half-demons and demons nearby—was that how he had enchanted the amulets to find the half-demons?

I shook my head and flipped to the next one.

Bingo.

The Bloodsbane ritual. It was a dark ritual where the user took a human sacrifice to a tainted place. He then brutally killed the human, a witch, and a demon in a bloody ceremony in order to harness their energy and power. It gave the user extraordinary magic and immortal life.

My gut twisted in disgust as I read the details.

This was it, though. This was how Randall was able to wield magic and live for so long.

The chapter went on, explaining more technical parts of the ritual. It had to be performed every full moon, and the user's magic drained off as the month went by. If not performed for a few full moons, the user lost all magic and would start to age.

I was sure not many in the demon hunter community knew about this ritual, but I could bet my place at this academy, they would say this ritual was illegal and highly forbidden if they found out.

If the other demon hunters found out Randall was performing this ritual, he would certainly lose his position as the headmaster of the academy, if not worse. Knowing some of the demon hunters in our society, I was sure they would call for Randall's death.

I pulled my phone from my pocket and snapped pictures of the book's pages. When the time came, I could use these as evidence.

I had done it. I would now be able to destroy Randall and finish my deal with Crimson.

I flipped the pages until it was open to the same page as before I arrived, and I retreated from the back room and out the library. I locked the door with my magic and hurried downstairs.

"What are you up to, Rey?"

His voice sent a chill down my spine. I turned bond found Randall standing to the side in the building's foyer.

"I was in my office, grading papers," I lied, rolling my shoulders, as if I was too tired and sore from being hunched over my desk for so long. "I lost track of time."

Randall stalked to me, his dark eyes locked on mine.

"Funny. I went by your office a little bit ago, but it was locked."

I frowned. "It must have been when I went out for a snack." Fuck, this was getting worse. I had to turn this around fast. I checked my phone. It was just past eleven at night. "What are you doing here at this time of the night?"

Randall flashed me a smile. "You know it's forbidden to have cell phones on campus."

"And you know I carry it with me often," I rebuked. "Are you going to take it away from me now?"

He waved me off. "Of course not, just don't let the students see it, or they will argue about it."

I nodded. "I won't." I slipped my phone back into my pocket. "I should get going."

"Right." Randall showed me a fake grin. "You should go rest for the night."

The tone of his voice, the glint in his eyes, that fucking grin ... he knew I was up to something.

I wouldn't cave in so easily. "Good night."

"Good night," Randall said.

I walked out of the building and turned right, to the Dahlia Villa. I wanted to go check on Erin before I retreated into my townhouse for the night, but I didn't trust Randall not to be following me right now. I couldn't show him I could shift into a raven, or that I cared that much about Erin.

So I tucked my fucking tail between my legs and marched to my near-empty house.

Once inside, I turned on the lights and let out a long breath.

What the fuck? Where had he been while I was in his library? Had Randall seen me in there? Had he been waiting for me in the foyer to scare me shitless?

I shook my head. He wouldn't dare do something to me right now. It would be too suspicious, too sudden.

Letting my thoughts simmer through all I had learned tonight, I took a warm shower, put on black pajama pants, and went to the kitchen to get something to eat.

Because I spent most of my spare time in raven form watching out for Erin, I had been skipping many of my meals, which meant I was always starving at this time of the night.

Not really in the mood to cook, I grabbed a dulce de leche ice cream tub from the freezer, sat down on the tall stool in front of the kitchen island, and dug in.

A knock came from the door.

I almost dropped my spoon.

"What the fuck?" I muttered, resting the ice cream on top of the island.

I dragged my bare feet to the door. These fucking townhouses didn't have a peephole, and I surely didn't want to use my magic to see who was outside. Channeling my power, just in case, I opened the door.

My jaw hit the floor.

"Hey," Erin muttered. Her golden eyes ran the length of me before locking on my left pectoral, where the soul bond was imprinted on my skin. A red tint appeared over her cheeks.

Fuck, I was shirtless.

The fucking soul bond was apparent.

That hadn't been in my plans.

Well, she wasn't too bad either in jean shorts that showed off her lean legs, and a purple blouse with a wide neckline that fell over one of her shoulders. Her long hair was loose and a few strands moved when a gentle breeze flew by.

Fighting the urge to cross my arms, I asked, "What are

you doing here?" Realizing it was probably midnight and she had crossed campus alone, fury swirled in me. "Are you crazy? What if Tom or some of the other half-demon-hating motherfuckers found you?"

"I know it was irresponsible, but I really wanted to tell you something."

I frowned. "Erin, whatever it is, it's none of my business. You know I don't want to get involved in whatever happens with you."

She flinched. "I just ..." She shook her head. "It was stupid. You're right. I just let the knowledge that you had helped me so many times before, that you knew what was going on with me when not even I knew, trick my mind and feelings. I thought you could help me this time too." She took a step back. "Sorry to bother you."

She turned to leave.

Fuck. Now I was curious about whatever the problem was. I mean, if it was a big problem, I definitely wanted to know and help, even if I would rather she didn't know about my involvement.

Moreover, I wouldn't send her away by herself this late at night.

"Erin, wait." I took a step to the side, opening the door some more. "Come in."

She glanced at me, her eyes narrowed. Without a word, she came in. She followed me to the kitchen, where I offered her a clean spoon.

She took it. "What's this for?"

I gestured to the ice cream tub. "So you can eat with me while you tell me what's going on."

Her brows curled down and she set the spoon down. "I'm good. Thanks."

I took my place in the stool and fished a spoonful of ice cream. "So, what's the problem?"

The knot between her brows deepened. "I've learned that King Brikan has children around the world."

Fuck. My appetite gone, I let go of the ice cream and pushed my fork aside. "When did you learn that?"

"The other night." She averted her eyes. "My mother told me about it a couple of nights ago." From the way she was avoiding looking at me, I guessed it was during one of their hidden practices. Erin didn't know I knew about those, so I wouldn't question it.

This time, I crossed my arms, puzzled. "Why are you coming to me?"

"Because I think I need to find them," she said, her voice wistful. "If I can convince them to join me, my chances—*our* chances—of defeating the supreme demon are much greater. But ... my mother is against the idea. And Claire also expressed concern about looking for them. So I'm on my own, and I don't know where to start."

I saw where this was going. "You want my help locating them."

She nodded. "I thought about locating spells, but all the ones I could find need something from the person you're trying to find, and since I don't know them, I have nothing. I thought that maybe you knew another way."

"Why is your mother against it?"

This clearly hit a sensitive spot as Erin's jaw hardened for a moment before she spoke. "She says King Brikan's children aren't all children. Some will be old, some will be young. But most of all, she thinks most don't know who they are and what they can do, and they won't want to join me. She thinks it's a waste of time."

I nodded. "I agree with most of that, but not the part where it's a waste of time."

Her golden eyes bulged. "So you'll help me?"

Her excitement gutted me. Holy fuck, how I was dying to reach over, to pull her to me, and show her how much I could help her.

I cleared my throat. "I can't promise anything, but I'll research another way of locating a person."

A smile tugged at the corners of her lips. "Thank you."

I lowered my gaze, afraid of being pulled in by her charm, but something else made me stiffen. I stood from the stool and reached to her collarbone, where a thin chain rested against her skin with a small, silver, coin-like pendant. I pulled it from underneath her blouse. "Randall's amulet. You're still wearing it."

She shrugged. "My contract with him is still valid, even if he hasn't called on me for a while now. Better to wear it all the time than to risk taking it off and having him do something to you."

I stared into her pretty, enchanting eyes. She was still wearing that thing for me, because she made a deal with Randall for me, to save me. Why did we keep saving each other? Why were we linked like that?

My hand traveled to the side, my fingertips pushing her blouse aside some more, until the soul bond was visible.

This. This was what linked us. What practically made us one.

A mirror of myself, Erin raised her hand and splayed her palm over the mark on my chest.

"Don't," I hissed.

She took a small step forward, practically erasing the

distance between us. She lifted her chin, lining her mouth up with mine.

"Then pull away," she whispered.

I was ensnared in her web and she knew it. I couldn't move, I couldn't say anything, because if I opened my mouth, it would be to confess my real feelings.

Rising on her tiptoes, Erin snaked her other hand around my shoulders and tugged me toward her. Powerless, I leaned into her.

She pressed her lips to mine, and I let out a sigh—a relieved and satisfied sound I knew I couldn't disguise.

Lost in her, I cradled the nape of her neck and kissed her.

13

ERIN

I KNEW Rey wasn't made of steel. I knew I could get to him. The problem was making him stay with me.

When his lips crashed against mine, demanding more, I didn't think of anything else. Even if he only kissed me for a second, then pushed me away, I would take whatever I could.

Because I loved him and I needed him.

Right now.

I parted my lips, letting him in. Mmm, his lips tasted of ice cream, and I wished I could eat him up.

Then Rey took control.

One of his arms wound around my waist and he twirled us, lifting me a little and depositing me on top of the tall stool, my back against the kitchen island. He stepped between my legs, and I took advantage of that to wrap my legs around his hips, trapping him with me. He moved his hips against me, and I let out a gasp, feeling how much he wanted this.

How much he desired me.

While he kissed me senseless, I glided my hands over his

back, his shoulders, and his arms, taking in all the muscles in his hot, hot body. I had seen him without a shirt before, and we had kissed before, but both had never happened at the same time. I wanted to imprint all the valleys and mountains of his body in my memory. I wished I could touch him like that all the freaking time.

Suddenly, he broke the kiss, but before my desperation flowered, his lips moved to my jaw and down my neck. He licked, bit, and grazed his teeth along my skin, leaving a trail of fire that traveled deep inside me, heating my entire body.

His hands slipped under my blouse, and this time he didn't hesitate. His hand closed around one of my breasts, his fingertips dipping inside my bra.

Holy shit ... My back arched and I was sure I was close to dying in his hands.

I lowered my hands around his back and paused for a moment, afraid he would push me away again, but when I reached for the waist of his pants, he didn't stop me. I lowered his pants an inch, so I could feel that thrilling V that lined his six pack, then slid my hand under his pants.

Behind us, his phone rang with a new message, startling us.

Rey jumped back several feet, his eyes wide.

Cold seeped into my body instantly, not only from missing his body against mine, but because I knew what came next. I knew what he would do.

Running a hand through his hair, Rey turned his back to me.

Tears filled my eyes, but I wiped them, determined that he wouldn't see them.

"You should go," he said, his voice low.

I hopped off the stool, completely humiliated. "Why do you do this?"

He turned to me, clearly confused. "Do what?"

Was he going to act like he had amnesia? "Kiss me until I'm dazed, then push me away."

"This is my fault?" he asked, sounding shocked. "You're the one provoking me!"

I gasped. What the hell? I straightened my shirt. "You say you don't want anything with me, then you press me against walls or floors or counters." I gestured to the island behind me "Even if I provoke you, as you say I do, ignore me. Push me away from the start. Because the way it is right now, it seems you're just using me then pushing me away."

"I'm using you?"

I shook my head, a turmoil of emotions clouding my mind, clogging my veins. "I have one question for you, Rey, just one question. Do you like me?" He opened his mouth to answer, but I continued, "And don't spout that crap that we can't be together because of this or that. Even if we can't be together, I just want to know, do you like me?"

His nostrils flared. "No, Erin, I don't."

It was a knife to my heart. "I see." I nodded as tears burned behind my eyes. "So you have been using me because you know I like you." I inhaled deeply. "I shouldn't have come here. I shouldn't have asked for your help. I'm sorry for bothering you."

I walked past him.

I half expected him to stop me, to call me back, to come after me and say he was joking.

But he didn't.

He remained rooted to the same spot even when I paused

at the front door and said, "I'm sorry about the soul bond. If there was a way of breaking it, I would do it."

I opened the door and left his townhouse.

It was probably after one in the morning, and at this time of night, it was getting chilly. Why had I worn damn shorts when it was starting to get a bit cooler? Oh, I knew, because I had wanted to seduce him. I had hoped he would see me, want me, and lose control.

I had provoked him, like Rey had accused me of.

But that was over. I was done with all of it. I wasn't going to go looking for him anymore, asking for help, or even go to his classes. I didn't care if I failed and couldn't graduate. It wasn't like I dreamed of being a full-fledged demon hunter.

My dream for the future was to survive my doomed fate.

Afraid of being out alone in the middle of the night, I ran to the Gardenia building on the other side of campus. When I got closer to the entrance, I saw a raven perched in the same spot as the other night. Was it the same one?

Who cared?

Shaking my head, I entered the building and rushed to my bedroom, where I fell in my bed and buried my face in my pillow.

Surprisingly, I didn't cry.

"Erin, wake up."

A hand shook my shoulder. I slapped that hand away. "Let me sleep."

"I'm worried." Claire sat on the bed, pushing me to the side. "Are you okay? It's almost noon and you're still in bed. That's not normal."

It was freaking Saturday. I could sleep until whatever shitty time I wanted.

I covered my head with my pillow. "Shh, it's too loud in here."

"Are you drunk?"

I chuckled, the sound muffled by the pillow. "I wish."

Claire pulled the pillow away from me. "What happened?"

I shook my head. "I really don't want to talk about it."

Claire's eyebrows hiked up. "And you know I'll bug you until you spill the beans."

Groaning, I rolled to my side and closed my eyes. "Last night, I was panicking. I had this sudden need to do something about King Brikan's other children, but I didn't know where to start. Shit, it was so freaking stupid of me."

"What did you do?" Worry laced her words.

"I went to Rey." I sat up. "Stupid, right? I wasn't even aware it was so late. I just ... had to do something. And he had helped so much before. Finding out about this mark." I touched the mark on my wrist. "Training me with my magic, closing the portal." Well, technically, I had helped him close the portal, but he had done it because of me. Or at least I thought that was case until last night. I didn't know anything anymore. "So many things. I thought that, even though he didn't want to be with me, you know, romantically, he was a good guy who wanted to help out and do what was right."

"I'm guessing he didn't want to help you this time."

I shook my head. "No, he did. He said he would research how to locate my siblings for me. But then ... we kissed and I thought ..."

"You would have sex?"

My cheeks warmed. "Yes. I thought he had finally given

in, but as usual, he ended up pushing me away before things progressed. But worse than that was his answer to my question."

"What question?"

"If he liked me. He said no."

Claire frowned. "I'll be the first to admit that is odd. I always thought Rey was holding back because of something else, like honor, or like because he thought being around him put you in more danger."

"The last one was the professor thing. He's a professor; I'm a student."

"Oh, yeah, that too." She tsked. "But he said he didn't like you? Are you sure he wasn't lying?"

I shrugged. "Does it matter? He looked straight at me and said he didn't like me. I'm done with him. Even if I'm dying and he's the only one who can help me, I won't go to him. I'm completely done with him."

"Oh, Erin." Claire hugged me. "That must have hurt. I know how much that hurts." I hugged her back, both of us mourning relationships that had barely started.

How I wished Claire would take notice of Harper, who was completely starstruck, and move on. As for me, I was seriously considering becoming a nun.

"Is there such thing as a demon hunter nun? Or maybe a demonic princess nun?"

Claire pulled back, a puzzled look on her face. "Both titles sound fun, but unlikely to happen."

I let out a long sigh. "I know. I'm just ... I'm done. That's all. No Rey, no guys. At least for a long while." I rubbed my chest, right above a certain mark. "I wish there was a way to break the soul bond, so it would be easier to move on, you know?"

"You don't mean that," Claire said, her voice low.

"I do." I nodded. "What good is this bond if he's completely ignoring it? There's no reason to be linked for life like this if we won't be together. I bet that if I didn't have this mark on my chest, I wouldn't feel so drawn to him, I wouldn't feel the need to seek him out. Life would be simpler."

"If you say so," Claire said, clearly unconvinced.

Maybe I wasn't either, but that was only one way to work this through.

I puffed my chest. "From now on, I should focus on studying, and practicing, and finding King Brikan's children."

"That spells research, and I love research." Claire hopped off my bed. "Come on. Get dressed. Let's have lunch and then hit the library. We need to find a spell to locate your siblings."

I glanced out the window. The sun was high and bright, promising a beautiful day. Spend one of the last warm Saturdays of the seasons stuck in the library? It wasn't as if I had anything else to do.

I jumped out of bed. "Sounds like a plan."

14

———

REY

As a raven, I was perched on the roof of the Aster building, waiting for Randall. The full moon was back, and I was certain he would soon walk out of the building, wearing his long cloak, and head into the woods.

And I would follow him again. But this time, I was going to enter the portal with him. I had stashed my phone inside my pocket before shifting to record it all.

If Randall really performed the Bloodsbane ritual, or anything like that, it would be his end.

From here, I could get a glimpse of the Gardenia building. A couple of hours earlier, I had seen Erin entering her room through her window, with Claire and Harper. The three of them ate chocolate while talking. While Claire and Harper seemed animated, Erin was putting on a show. Whenever they weren't looking, her smile faded and her shoulders sagged. She had been like that ever since that night at my house a couple of weeks before.

She hadn't showed up to my class anymore, which to be honest was good for me, because I wasn't sure I could handle being in closed quarters with her again. She was a walking temptation and my control was fading. Even with her mother's threat hanging over my head.

But her absence made me a little worried. How would she graduate if she failed my class? By now, I should have reported her for skipping, but I was hoping a miracle would happen, and things would resolve themselves.

I hadn't seen her face-to-face anymore, but I still followed her around when I thought it was necessary. Despite knowing we could never be, my feelings for her only got stronger every single day, and my need to make sure she was okay consumed me if I didn't check on her every few hours.

I felt like a complete motherfucker for putting that permanent frown on her pretty face. I wished we lived another life, where she wasn't a demonic princess and I wasn't a half-demon. We could have met under normal circumstances, while we both attended college, fallen in love between classes and parties, and lived happily ever after together.

Why the fuck I was thinking about that? These thoughts only made me hurt more.

Finally, when it was almost midnight, Randall walked out of the building. Like a month ago, he simply strolled through the academy, and no one crossed his path, no one saw him. At the outpost, the guards marched a few feet away and turned their backs, as if enchanted, and only after Randall had crossed through the gates, they woke up and returned to their post.

I followed Randall through the forest, to the same spot I had seen him before. He chanted some words under his breath, and the portal appeared under the same arched tree trunk. He walked in.

I sucked in a sharp breath and followed him in.

The portal opened to faint sunshine over a wintery scenery. Snow covered the ground and the treetops, and a small, old, ramshackle cottage sat a few feet away. Randall walked into the cottage.

Where the fuck were we? The book said the ritual had to take place in a tainted place. Could this be Randall's first home? Where demons killed his family? I didn't know the details, no one knew, but I had heard rumors about it.

I flew closer and peeked through a window, the glass broken and jagged. Randall stood inside what looked like the main room of the cottage, and three figures cowered before him. All three of them had chains around their wrists, ankles, and neck that connected to a newer concrete wall in the back of the cottage.

I shifted into my human form and crouched lower.

Randall paced before the three figures, making it hard to see them, but by now I was sure what or who they were. A human, a witch, and a demon. Just like the book described.

I fished my phone from my pocket and started recording.

"Please," the female human cried. "You don't want to do this. Please let us go."

Randall halted before her. He had his back to me, but I could bet he was snickering at her. Without a word, Randall summoned his Dawnblade and slit the woman's throat, just above the metal band around her neck.

Blood oozed from the cut as she tried speaking, tried crying. Gurgling sounds filled the room. The woman's body fell forward, the chains keeping her from crumpling to the ground.

Beside her, the witch screamed and retreated as much as the chains would let her. "Randall, don't do this, please."

"It's for a noble cause, Brielle."

Wait ... he knew this witch? How? And why was he killing her if he knew her?

Randall caught the witch by the hair, pulled her head up, and slashed her throat.

Then he turned to the demon.

The muttmaug demon snarled at Randall, as if he could put the demon hunter off with his sharp teeth and his big, curling horns. Randall wasn't fazed. Not getting too close, he stabbed the demon's chest with his blade. The demon roared, shaking the cottage. A half-broken window next to the one I was hiding fell and broke on the floor. I lowered myself behind the wall, in case Randall looked this way.

My heart hammering in my chest, I counted to ten, then went back to the window.

Randall had already pulled his sword out and slit the demon's throat.

His three victims were dead.

Next, Randall stood back and looked down. I had to stand up to see what he was staring at.

A pentagram was etched on the cottage's floor, and it now filled with the blood seeping from the three bodies. When the grooves of the pentagram were full, Randall picked up a golden chalice and used it to take a little of the blood from the human, the witch, and the demon.

Holding the chalice, Randall stepped into the center of the pentagram. He brought the chalice high and began speaking in a demonic language.

It was a prayer of sorts, asking the powers of the universe, the gods if they existed, to give him ultimate power and eternal life.

Red light shone from the pentagram, bathing the place with the color and scent of blood.

Then, Randall drank from the chalice.

Blood slid down Randall's mouth, to his neck, staining his clothes. With arms open wide, Randall let out a satisfied gasp, as if he had just satiated an incredible thirst.

My stomach turned and my hands shook, barely able to keep the camera straight.

Like snakes, the red light swirled up, circling Randall.

It was working. He was gaining more power and immortal life. Randall smiled, satisfied. Powerful. Immortal.

The lights faded.

The ritual was done, but Randall wasn't.

He stepped forward and unchained the three bodies. He grabbed the arm of the human and dragged her back to the concrete wall. I lost sight of him for a moment, but I changed windows and saw a heavy metal door on the concrete wall.

Randall opened it. The groans and shrieks of demons burst through the opening. I could see their claws trying to swipe at Randall. But he simply raised his hand and the demons retreated, as if they were being pushed by an invisible shield.

Randall threw the human body among the demons. They fell over the body, devouring it like piranhas. I pressed a hand over my mouth before I spilled my guts on the ground. I had seen plenty in my long life, and I thought nothing else could make me sick or repulsed.

I had been wrong.

Randall repeated the process with the other two bodies. Then, he locked the metal door and wiped his hands on his cloak.

And I crouched again.

I was done with all of this. Even if he did more, even if he killed more, drank more blood, whatever, I had recorded enough.

I pocketed my phone, shifted into a raven, and flew out of there.

My first instinct was to find Crimson and give the video to him right away. If I showed this to Crimson or the school board, Randall was done for. But I wanted leverage over Crimson too. I could do this for him, and he could still threaten Erin—or worse.

Instead, I went back to my townhouse, where I took a long, long shower, as if I could wash those terrible images from inside my mind, and then paced my room, thinking.

I would wait awhile more to show this to someone. Didn't the ritual have to be performed whenever there was a full moon, and Randall's powers drained as the month progressed? I would act when Randall was at his weakest.

Only then would the academy have a chance of surviving him once I exposed the gruesome truth. Because I was sure Randall wouldn't go down quietly.

15

ERIN

THE RESEARCH about how to locate my siblings wasn't going well. Claire and I met at the library several times a week, but it seemed no book in there was about those spells. The restricted area probably had it, but I wasn't up to sneaking into it—at least not yet. Claire had also searched her father's books and found nothing.

Meanwhile, I also researched how to break the soul bond.

A few weeks had gone by since my last encounter with Rey. Now that I wasn't going to his class, I hadn't seen him at all, and that made me both relieved and utterly sad.

I missed him. That was a fact. I missed everything we were and could have been. The few times we lowered our guards and had a real conversation or worked together, we had been great. We had been more than great. We had been perfect together. This soul bond wasn't a joke. We were soul-mates; I knew and I felt that.

But that wasn't enough.

I wouldn't force him to be with me if he didn't want to.

However, the search for a way to break the soul bond was

going even worse than the first one. Every book Claire and I found was vehement that the bond couldn't be broken.

One morning before my other magical beings class, I sat down on the bench under the blackthorn tree. It was still early and the campus was quiet. There were no demon hunter students out to bother me yet. I leaned back on the bench, enjoying the serene start of the day, even if I had to tighten my jacket in the chilling weather. If I wasn't mistaken, the forecast was for snow soon. I wasn't ready for that.

Though nothing in my life was going as I hoped, I tried taking breaks when I could to appreciate the little things. I hadn't done this in a while.

I'd never had reasons to believe in God or any other deity, and my aunt hadn't told me about any or taught me about anything like that. To be honest, I had no idea if demon hunters worshipped a god, or many, or none.

So, I looked up at the twisting, thorny branches of the blackthorn tree. I wasn't sure if it was because it had given me a Dawnblade, but I felt connected to it. Maybe this tree was my deity.

Staring at the many thorns all over its branches and trunk, I wondered ... what would my life be like right now if I hadn't been so stupid and volunteered for that dare? If I hadn't walked into the haunted house. If Aunt Paula wasn't dead.

Would I still be stuck in Spring Hill? Would I still be living with Aunt Paula? Would I have finally run away? Gone to college? Found a job?

Found a human guy who actually liked me and treated me well?

For some reason, I doubted it. Knowing what I knew now, I was sure it was just a matter of time before my doomed fate found me. There had to be a reason why my aunt and I moved closer and closer to the academy, right? To be near this place when all the chaos ensued.

I was sure she, and my mother for that matter, hadn't planned for everything to go down so soon, but they knew it would happen, sooner or later.

The campus started waking up, and students walked from the dorms to the other buildings for class.

Soon, Claire halted before me. "I knew I would find you here. Everything okay?"

Nothing was okay, but I had to trudge on, hadn't I?

I nodded at her. "It will be."

She beckoned for me to get up from the bench. "Come on before we're late for class."

Feeling slightly less bummed than before, I dragged my feet to our other magical beings class with Claire. Ava was in this class too, but she hadn't been sitting with us lately. She had gone back to being the blond bitch and sitting with Stella and Ruby a couple of rows in front of us.

Professor Adeline, a tall, lean woman with long blue hair who apparently despised the half-demons, started the class a second after the last student came inside the classroom.

"Today we'll talk about witches," she said. While lecturing, she always looked at all the full-blooded demon hunters, ignoring my kind completely. I tried not to let that get to me and pay attention to the class. "There are several covens here in North America, but the most powerful ones are the Silverblood, the Bluemoon, Blackmarsh, the Wildthorn, and the Bonecrown covens."

She went on explaining their differences, like different magic, different customs, and different habitats. She told us that the current queen of the Silverblood coven, Thea, married Drake, the vampire lord of DuMoir Castle, the most powerful vampire coven on this side of the globe, forming an alliance between not only witches and vampires, but also werewolves.

Their daughter, Aurora, was a unique being. Before her birth, an old witch told them that Aurora was the next Queen of All Witches—a title given to the most powerful of all witches. The Queen of All Witches was supposed to rule above all other witches, regardless of their coven.

But it was when she got to the Wildthorn coven that my interest piqued.

"One of the unique powers of the Wildthorn witches is the ability to break any curse or bond," the professor said.

Claire and I exchanged a glance. What? They could break any bond? Like the soul bond? So all I had to do was find the Wildthorn witches? I knew that wouldn't be easy, but it was a start. A direction.

I almost raised my hand and asked if the professor knew if any of those witches had a locator spell that didn't require something from the missing person, but I remained quiet. We had learned one thing, at least.

The professor dismissed the class, and I rushed to her desk. I knew she didn't like the half-bloods, but as a professor under the headmaster's orders to treat all of us well until the Shadow Trials, she had to be nice to me, right?

"Yes?" she asked as I halted in front of her desk. Claire was right by my side.

"Professor, I was wondering, these witches, do they live close by?"

She narrowed her eyes at me. "The powerful covens? No, they all live in the north."

My chest deflated. "So, no Wildthorn nearby?"

"No," she said, her voice taut. "If there are, they are strays in hiding. Unless a demon hunter is hunting them on purpose, there's no way of finding them." She lifted her chin. "Is that all?"

I could tell when I was being dismissed. "Yes. Thank you."

"That was a bummer," Claire said as we left the classroom.

"Maybe we can research the Wildthorn witches," I suggested. "Maybe we can find clues to their location in the books."

"But you heard the professor," Claire said. "The coven is up north. Unless you're planning on leaving for several days, I think that's a waste of time."

"What do you want with Wildthorn witches?" Claire and I turned and faced Ava in the middle of the hallway. I opened my mouth, not sure what I would say, but Ava shook her head. "You know what? I don't care."

"What do you mean?" I asked, a little wary of Ava. Sometimes she reminded of Rey with the hot and cold thing. In one situation, we were beating each other up, in another, we were working together as if we were great partners.

"I know where you can find Wildthorn witches."

"How?" Claire asked.

"One of my father's tasks is to find Wildthorn witches who stray south and kill them."

"Where can we find them?" I asked.

"You think I'm giving you the information for free?" she asked, appalled. "No, I want a favor first."

Oh, there was a catch. I shifted my weight. "What is it?"

She looked around, to make sure no one was close by to listen to us. "I need your help with Harvey. He doesn't notice me at all, and I'm tired of chasing after him. I want him to come to me. But I need a plan for that. I want you to help me come up with and execute a plan that will make him fall head over heels for me."

"What about your friends, Stella and Ruby?" I asked. "Why won't they help?"

"I didn't ask them." Ava pressed her lips together. "They wouldn't understand, okay?" She shook her head. "You don't either. This is a waste of breath." She started to turn.

I grabbed her wrist. "Wait. I understand." I glanced at Claire, who nodded at me, before returning my eyes to Ava. "We can help you."

"You can?" Ava sounded suspicious. "Why?"

Claire shrugged. "Because we like helping."

Ava didn't seem convinced, but on with it. "All right. Help me win Harvey's heart, and I'll tell you where to find the Wildthorn witches."

I was excited about the prospect of finding the witch and breaking the soul bond. Only problem was, how would we make Harvey fall for Ava?

16

I HAD JUST FINISHED TEACHING a class—one that Erin should have been in—and students were filing out when Vaira walked in. Since the outing of the Black Knight Unit and the half-demons, she had become sort of their leader. The direct contact with Randall. At first, I felt betrayed, but that lasted only two seconds. I was glad she was in charge of them instead of me. I had enough on my plate as it was.

Besides, after what I found out about Randall, I was glad he didn't ask me to do things as much. I had always thought he was hiding something, something bad, but I had no idea it was plain evil. Everyone was afraid of King Brikan when another big bad was under their noses.

Everyone was in for a big surprise.

With a superior air, Vaira halted in front of my desk. "I came to ask for the favor you owe me."

I knew this day would come. "And what would that favor be?"

She shifted her weight, as if she was nervous about this

conversation. "Convince Randall to call off the Shadow Trials."

I frowned. "I already asked him to do that, and he shut me out."

"Because you didn't beg?"

As if begging would help. "Look, Vaira, I haven't been close to Randall in months. I would say the best person to ask him to cancel the contest is you."

"I've already asked him," she muttered. "This isn't what we signed up for, Rey. In fact, have you looked around lately?" She gestured to the windows overlooking the courtyard. "We are mistreated and disrespected left and right. Do you know how hard it is to keep a bunch of half-demon from lashing out? This is too much!"

I let out a long breath. "I know, and I'm sorry. I never intended for all of this to happen." If I had known all the trouble it would cause, perhaps I would have convinced Randall not to pursue the half-demons.

She leaned over the table. "You might not have had bad intentions, but it is your fault we got roped into this mess."

"Hey, I'm as blindsided as you are," I told her. "Randall told me I'll have to participate in the Shadow Trials, so believe me, I want it called off as much as you do."

"You'll have to participate?" She shook her head. "I thought you were his favorite."

I snorted. "He only pretends that." Why, I wasn't so sure. "Oh, and when I talked to him, he told me the contest will be out of his hands soon. He asked the full-fledged hunters to handle it."

"Fuck," she hissed.

I wondered ... I had asked Randall to call off the contest, but with Crimson's thirst for power and my video, he wouldn't be headmaster for long. Crimson would, and he wouldn't allow such a contest to be run by the full-fledged demon hunters, not when he would have snatched the headmaster mantle. He would want to do it all himself. Or, if I played my cards well, he could simply take it back from the demon hunters and run it himself.

Or not run it at all.

"If, and only if, I can get the Shadow Trials called off, my favor will be paid off, right?" I asked Vaira.

She narrowed her eyes. "Yes. But you just said you tried and Randall said no."

One corner of my lips tugged up. "I might know another way."

ON MY WAY to the Aster building, I caught sight of Erin, Claire, and Ava seated on a bench under the blackthorn tree, their backs to me. My steps faltered at seeing Erin when I wasn't expecting to, but also at seeing Ava with her. I hadn't seen the three of them together in a long while. Was Ava their friend again? I had lost count of how many times I saw them together and then not.

I shouldn't care, but I did, because to keep Erin safe, I had to know who she was hanging out with. And now Ava seemed to be on the table again.

All right, Erin was fine for now, so I pushed forward and plodded to the Aster building. As I expected, Professor Crimson was in his office, seated behind his desk, messing with some papers.

When he saw me, he put the papers away and locked inside a drawer under his desk.

"Rey, what brings you here?" he asked, his voice too cheery for my taste.

"I've got it," I told him.

Crimson stilled. "You've got what?"

He knew what I was talking about. "I've got evidence to get Randall fired, or even to have him executed. You'll soon be headmaster of this academy."

Slowly, Crimson stood. "What is it? Where is it?"

He really thought I would hand it to him that easily? I shook my head. "I'll reveal Randall's secret and destroy him when the time is right, but only if you agree to call off the Shadow Trials."

Crimson's jaw ticked. "What? Are you trying to bargain with me?"

"Yes, I am." I puffed out my chest. I wasn't one bit afraid of Crimson, never had been, but I sure was afraid of what he could do to Erin. "You promise me you'll forget about Erin, and when you're headmaster, you'll cancel the Shadow Trials right away, and in a couple of weeks, I'll help you destroy Randall."

Crimson narrowed his eyes at me, thinking. "You're asking for more than we first agreed."

"Because the evidence I have is good," I told him. "It won't leave any margin for error. Randall will be gone soon, and you'll take over the school. If you agree to my terms."

Crimson's hand curled, the knuckles turning white. I could see he wanted to yell at me, maybe even strike me somehow, but his hands were tied. "All right. I'll make that deal in order to become headmaster. I won't touch Erin and I'll call off the Shadow Trials. But you better come through, Rey. Or else ..."

Or else.

I knew exactly what *or else* meant.

"Good," I said.

Without anything else to share, I left Crimson's office and let out a long breath of relief. Things seemed to be going in the right direction. Randall, that horrible monster, would be dealt with, the Shadow Trials would be canceled, and Erin would be safe.

At least from Crimson.

AVA'S IDEA WAS RIDICULOUS. Claire and I had told her it was overkill and gave her some other options, but she didn't listen. She was sure her idea would work.

She had told us Harvey usually ran at the track behind the Hyacinth building three times a week, and he came back the long way around the buildings, walking by the side of the Snapdragon building in the process.

So, one evening after our classes, Claire and I hid behind some bushes on the side of the Snapdragon building, Ava hid behind some trees a few feet from us, and we waited.

Ava kept checking her wristwatch, while Claire played on her phone—the one she shouldn't have with her.

"What?" She shrugged. "I only brought it because I thought this would be boring. I was right."

I chuckled.

But a moment later, Ava shushed us. "He's coming," she whispered.

Harvey appeared from behind the building, wearing

shorts and a t-shirt with large sweat spots that clung to his torso, and walked by the side of the male dorm building.

"Now," Ava mouthed.

On cue, I channeled my magic and called upon the zombie creatures with ease. Werewolves, vampires, and other supernaturals jumped out of the shadows and charged Harvey.

He froze for a moment, his eyes wide in confusion, but then he shook the daze off and called his Dawnblade. I conjured more zombies, more than he could handle by himself.

That was when Ava, the savior, appeared. Dawnblade in hand, she lunged at the zombies and fought her way to Harvey.

While Harvey was busy fighting for his life—or at least believing he was—Ava pretended to fight the zombies to save him. Whenever she got too close to one of them, I blinked them away, so it seemed like she was cutting through them like a freaking master.

She jumped, somersaulted, flipped, and twirled her sword as if she was practicing an ambitious choreography. Every one of her moves were exaggerated, unnatural.

My stomach twisted with awkwardness.

Finally, she stepped in front of the last zombie and swiped her blade wide, cutting across the zombie's chest. It faded away like smoke.

Ava turned to him, flipping her hair like an Amazon. "Are you okay?" A boisterous laughter burst from Harvey's throat. Ava frowned. "What the hell?"

"That was ... so funny." Harvey's Dawnblade disappeared and he placed a hand over his belly, laughing some more.

Ava paled. "What?"

Harvey rested a hand over her shoulder. "Whatever you were going for, Ava, it was a nice attempt. I have to give you props for that." He squeezed her shoulder, then walked away, still laughing.

Ava turned to us, her eyes wide, her jaw open. Claire and I inched from behind the bushes. "What was that?" Ava pointed in Harvey's direction with her blade.

"I'm guessing he caught on to what you were attempting," Claire said, trying not to laugh.

I wasn't laughing, but shit, that had been horrible—horribly funny and extremely awkward.

"How? I was saving his ass. He should have been thankful," Ava said, her tone high. "He should have looked at me as if I was his hero."

"Ava, think about it," I said. "Harvey is a good demon hunter. He knows how to fight and defend himself. He wouldn't be easily tricked." All things I had told her before, when she first explained her plan to us. Yet, she didn't listen.

"There were too many of them!" she argued.

I nodded. "Yes, but he must have known that zombified vampires and werewolves don't just simply wander around the campus grounds."

Groaning, Ava jutted her index finger at me. "This is your fault. Your zombies weren't convincing enough. You messed it up!"

I gaped at her. "It was your plan!"

"Whatever." Ava turned her chin up. "You failed, so I'm not telling you anything, especially not about the Wildthorn witches."

And just like that, she stomped away.

Stumped, I turned to Claire. "What the hell?"

Claire let out a small chuckle. "I can't believe she's mad at you."

"She promised to tell me where the Wildthorn witches are hiding." I shook my head, at a loss for what to do next. I guess Claire and I would have to go back to the drawing board—or the library.

"Just let her be," Claire said. "She'll calm down and you can ask her about the Wildthorn witches tomorrow. After all, you did help her."

Tomorrow? Ava wouldn't calm down that fast. Maybe next week. Or next month.

"What do you guys want with the Wildthorn witches?"

Claire and I turned in the direction of the new voice. Harper waltzed down the side path of the building.

"Harper," I said, a little wary. "What are you doing here?"

"Sorry, I didn't mean to hear anything," she said. "I was walking from the library to the Gardenia building, but then I caught sight of Harvey fighting a bunch of zombies. I was about to run in and help him, but then I saw Ava. She looked like an awkward, novice, action movie actress." A small smile adorned her lips. "Then I saw you two hiding and understood what was going on." She grew serious again. "But what is this about Wildthorn witches?"

Claire and I exchanged a glance. Though the entire academy hated me because of who what I was, Harper hadn't seemed to care about all that. She been a good friend so far. And she knew enough.

I let out a sigh. "We promised to help Ava in wooing Harvey in exchange for some info on where we could find Wildthorn witches."

Harper's smile widened. "That certainly didn't look like wooing."

Claire chuckled. "Awkward, novice, action movie actress. I love it! It's almost as great as the blond bitch."

"It was her idea," I said, a little disappointed. "But now that we failed, she won't tell us anything." I groaned. "We're back to square one."

Harper's brows knotted. "And why do you want to know where to find the Wildthorn witches?"

I pressed my lips together, thinking. Should I keep going and tell her more? Harper was alone most of the time; it wasn't as if she would tell anyone. Besides, she knew I was a half-demon and a demonic princess.

And she liked Claire, which meant, if someday Claire returned her feelings—one could only hope—Harper would be around us more. She would become an official member of our small gang. That thought actually made me glad.

"During class the other day, I learned that Wildthorn witches can break almost any curse or bond," I said. "Well, I have a soul bond with Rey, and I would like it gone."

Harper tilted her head. "You want it gone? Why? I thought you two liked each other."

I stared at her. "No, you got it wrong. I like him, but he doesn't like me."

"Are you sure?" she insisted.

Damn, even talking about this hurt. "Yes, he looked into my eyes and said so a few days ago."

"That is odd." She shook her head. "I could have sworn he was in love with you."

Claire shrugged. "I said the same thing."

"See, it wasn't just me," Harper said.

Their words only drove the knife deeper in my chest. "Unfortunately, you guys are mistaken. So, I want this bond gone."

"Well, if you're sure about that, I think I can help," she said.

Claire's eyes bugged. "You can?"

Harper dipped her chin once. "Yup. No one really knows this, but my grandmother is a Wildthorn witch."

"What? How?" I asked, not believing my ears.

"Yeah, she left her coven many decades ago when she fell in love with my grandfather, a demon hunter," Harper told us. "She left her customs and practices behind for him, but I know that after his death a few years ago, she rejoined them."

I gulped, afraid of my question. "You think she can break the soul bond?"

Harper shrugged. "I don't know but we can ask her."

"Right now?" Claire glanced at her phone. "It's almost time for dinner, then curfew." She paused. "Where does your grandmother live?"

"In Chasseur Ville," Harper said.

I tsked. "We wouldn't be able to go and come back before curfew."

"We can go this weekend," Harper suggested. "I'm sure she won't mind the visit."

I smiled at Harper. Though it hurt me to think I was taking another step to erase the bond between Rey and me, I was glad I was doing something. In the end, it would be for the best. I tried looking on the bright side of it all. At least now it seemed Harper was officially part of our small but tight group.

"It's a date." I winked at her.

Harper waved me off, but a small pink shade tinted her cheeks. Anything to spend more time with Claire, hm? I was glad that even though I wouldn't have my happily ever after, I could try to create one for them.

18

REY

IN THE PAST FEW DAYS, not only had I seen Erin walking around with Ava, and then Harper, but I had also seen her locked away in the library with Claire during their spare time. What the fuck were they up to? Every time Erin and Claire had spent hours over books, it had been to deal with bigger matters, evil demons, and such. Some of those times, I had participated, helping them with whatever they were facing.

I was desperate to know what they were researching, but I couldn't get close enough without being seen.

It was a fucking torment.

Although I didn't like leaving campus knowing Erin would be unprotected, I had to go pick up supplies for class at a witch's shop in West Hill. So, one evening, after seeing Erin through the window in Claire's room, I drove away.

But before driving to West Hill, I went to meet Vaira. I had visited her before, wanting to give her the news about the contest, and she had told me she was at a pub in Chasseur Ville.

An outed half-demon in a town full of demon hunters. Had she lost her fucking mind?

To my surprise, Vaira wasn't alone in the pub. Her boyfriend and leader of the half-camp settlement, Daerman, was with her. They were seated at a small table in the middle of the packed pub—full of humans ready to start the treasure hunt game.

I took a seat at their table.

"Vaira told me you were going to cancel this shitty contest," Daerman said, his voice not too low.

Eyes wide, I glanced around. What if the humans heard him? But no one seemed to be paying attention. The humans were way too excited about the rest of their evening.

I nodded. "Yes. I can't disclose details, but in a couple of weeks, the Shadow Trials will be canceled."

"That's great news," Vaira said. She raised her beer glass. "I'll count my favor paid once that's announced." She drank a long swallow of her drink. "Ah, great night to celebrate. Why don't you order one for yourself?"

As much as I wanted to, I didn't have time for that. "I can't. I have plans."

Daerman shot me a sly look. "Hm, plans? Who is the lucky girl?"

I fought the urge to roll my eyes. Almost one thousand years old and I still wanted to roll my eyes during some situations. "It isn't like that." I pushed my chair back.

Vaira smiled at me, the first smile she had offered me in a long time. "Thank you, Rey. I mean it."

"My pleasure." I dipped my head at both of them, then weaved through the crowd.

With a sense of mission accomplished, I left the pub, slipped into my car, and drove toward West Hill. It was one thing among so many others I had to work on, but I was glad to have that ticked off my to-do list.

Though West Hill was a quaint town at first glance, it was a pretty big dump. Past the beautiful greenway and the shops that surrounded it was a suburb that any human should be afraid to walk in.

I parked my car around the green and walked into the neighborhood. The cement of the sidewalk was cracked. The flowerbeds lining the sidewalks were either empty or filled with dead plants. The sides of the buildings served as murals for graffiti art, or showed the peeling of the paint, the collapsed concrete, the broken glass windows. It all looked as if it had been abandoned to rats and cockroaches.

The foul smell of rot and stuffy air of the place reached my nostrils, and I wrinkled my nose.

Five blocks later, I entered a dark alley.

The witch's shop was located at the end of the alley, where only the supernaturals would be able to locate it.

Halfway down the alley, I skidded to a halt.

The shop's black door opened and Professor Martha stepped out, a half open black bag in her arms.

"Rey." She cleared her throat. "I mean, Professor Rey. What brings you here?"

"I needed some herbs to enchant the swords for my class," I told her. My gaze fell to the bag in her arms and I frowned. "And why would you need hemlock and belladonna?"

I knew exactly why she needed them, and I was totally against it. Those herbs, and certainly the rest of the things inside the bag, were all used in dark magic. Like syphoning the lifeforce of dead bodies, or reanimating them.

"For my class," she said quickly. She taught magic spells,

and unless she wanted to go against the academy rules, she could only teach the students about benevolent spells.

All right, I was fucking tired of this pretense. "I know how you're using those." Her eyes widened. "Teaching dark magic to Erin? Are you fucking out of your mind?"

Martha's shock gone, she stilled herself, and her eyes hardened. "Have you been following us?" I pressed my jaw tight. "No, not us. You're following Erin."

Fuck. "What if I am?"

She stared at me for a moment, her eyes darkening. "I thought I made myself clear, Rey. Stay away from my daughter."

"I am staying away from her," I said through gritted teeth. "I just watch over her sometimes, from a distance." I inhaled deeply, and forced my voice to even out. "I'm following her to keep her safe," I said, my voice calm. Flat. "Or haven't you seen what Tom Heyward and his friends did to her?"

Martha glared at me. "I could beat that boy to a pulp, but … I don't need to, because you did, right? I heard the rumors that you punched Tom in the face."

I groaned. "I punched the wall beside his head, but I'm starting to regret that since I got in trouble for it anyway. Regardless, I won't allow that to happen again."

"No, *I* won't allow that to happen again. *I* will protect her." She took a step toward me. I was a head taller than her, but she didn't seem one bit fazed by my stature. "Last warning, Rey. Stay the fuck away from my daughter." I opened my mouth to tell her I wouldn't, but she went on, "Stay away from her, or I'll make you regret it."

I frowned, wondering why she hated me so much, what had I done to deserve such hatred. She didn't know how old I was or about my work for Asmodeus all those years, did she? She didn't. She couldn't know.

Unless Randall had told her. Or Erin. No, Erin wouldn't have done that.

With a humph, Martha marched past me and out of the alley.

My hands balled into fists and I felt an urge to go after her and ... I didn't even know what.

She was the mother of the woman I loved. If I decided to go against her, it would only make things worse. But at the same time, it was temptation. Was she serious? Was she really threatening me to stay away from Erin? Didn't she know it only enticed the demon in me?

I shook my head, sending those thoughts away. I couldn't worry about that now. Even without Martha's warning, I had no intention of getting close to Erin.

All right. I wasn't here for that. I walked to the door of the witch's shop, but stopped before I opened it.

Something caught my attention—a dark blue light.

Summoning my darkfire, I turned to it.

I gasped.

Three shiny, midnight blue werewolves stood in front of me. I had heard of them. They were the fabled Starlight pack, a pack of magical werewolves with incredible power. They had recently resurfaced after spending many years thought to be extinct.

One of the werewolves shapeshifted into a woman. She was pretty with long, brown curls and big hazel eyes. But what puzzled me was that when she shifted, clothes covered her body. I had never seen that trick before.

"Hi," the woman said. "I'm Luana, the alpha of the Starlight pack. I'm looking for my friend, Wyatt. I've been looking for him all over this region, and I heard rumors that he used to hang out with a half-demon named Reyan. That's you, right?"

I frowned. How the fuck did she know that? "I haven't heard from Wyatt in a while." Which was the truth. Last time I seen him? It was probably a year ago, when Erin had fled from the academy and ended up facing screinors. Wyatt had helped her, until he fainted from the screinors' powerful shriek.

She cursed under her breath. "It's a long story, but he is from my pack, before I became alpha. One day, he upped and left. No word, no news. I haven't heard from in almost two years. I need to know he's okay."

I shrugged. "Sorry, Luana, but I really don't know."

She shook her head. "If you hear from him, will you contact me?" She fished a cell phone from her pocket, and we exchanged numbers.

"Will do," I told her.

Luana shifted into a magical blue-purple werewolf, joined the other two, and they disappeared into the night.

I stayed put for a moment, wondering what might have happened to Wyatt. He had always been so quiet and predictable. Then suddenly, he disappeared and the pack's alpha was here looking for him. But Wyatt wasn't a Starlight wolf. I had seen him in wolf form many times, and he didn't glow as they did.

Wyatt was a big guy. An adult. Probably twenty-one years old? He could handle himself, I was sure. And if he couldn't, all he needed to do was ask for help.

Pushing him out of my mind, I walked into the store, eager to get this over with so I could get back to the academy. So I could check on Erin.

19

ERIN

FINALLY, the weekend was upon us. Saturday night I practiced with my mother. She had killed more mice and asked me to reanimate them. And we argued, as usual, because I didn't want to do that.

To appease her rage, I pretended to try, since she wouldn't know if I was really using magic or not, and in the end just told her I couldn't do it.

"I think these spells are out of my league," I said.

She didn't buy it, but she didn't push it either. Thankfully, she let me go after a few more tries.

On Sunday afternoon, Claire, Harper, and I piled into Claire's car and drove to Chasseur Ville. Harper told us she had called her grandmother to let her know she would be visiting with some friends. She hadn't told her grandmother any more details, and I was grateful for that. What if her grandmother was against people talking to her about her magic and her heritage? I didn't want to be shut down before even trying.

On the way there, I asked Harper about her lineage. "Do

you have any magic? I mean, you have at least a little Wildthorn blood in your veins."

She explained that technically she was twenty-five percent Wildthorn witch and yes, she had some magic, but it was all useless. She could make plants grow faster, and some other silly tricks. That was all.

Driving down the quaint streets of Chasseur Ville in the middle of the day, we passed the castle in the center of town. I looked up at it, right to the top of its roof, where Rey had taken me and where I first thought I could like him. That I was in danger of falling in love with him.

Back then, he was so caring, so friendly. There had been moments when he had avoided me, but not like now. Not like this.

Back then, I had believed he liked me too.

That felt like eons ago.

Following Harper's directions, Claire drove around the castle and into the more residential part of the village.

Not a minute later, Harper pointed to a two-story house with a wide, welcoming porch. Vines grew over the rails, and potted plants lined the driveway and crammed the house's entrance. "Here we are."

Claire brought her car into the driveway, and we exited it just as an old woman with short, white hair appeared at the door. A thin tiara of woven flowers sat atop of her head.

"Hello there," she said amiably. With a wide smile, she waited for us on the front porch. She wore a long dress with a colorful flower print. That and the tiara gave me the impression that she cared about her appearance.

That, or she was way into flowers and plants.

"Hi, Grandma." Harper embraced her tight, then turned to us. "These are my friends, Claire and Erin."

"It's a pleasure to have you all here," the old woman said.

"Thank you, ma'am," I said.

The old woman cracked a wide smile. "Ma'am? No, no, call me Francine. That's my name." She beckoned us forward. "Come on, I made cookies for you."

Harper's eyes widened. "If it's her honey cookies, they are the best."

The three of us followed Francine inside. The foyer opened to a living room dotted with even more plants than outside. I didn't know much about plants, but I could bet there were about a hundred different kinds spread through the house—entwined with the staircase's handrail, hanging from the ceiling, in vases on the corners, and over shelves, tables, and other furniture.

All right, it was definitely a plant thing.

"Please, take a seat," Francine said, gesturing to the brown leather couch in the middle of the living room. We sat down, and thirty seconds later, a large tray with many sweet-scented cookies appeared on the coffee table before us. "Please, dig in."

Harper advanced on the cookies, taking two. "These are my favorite," she said, before taking a huge bite of one of the cookies.

Francine chuckled. "I always have to hide them, or she'll eat them all."

"But it's so good," Harper muttered, her voice muffled by her full mouth.

I reached for one cookie and took a bite. My taste buds exploded. I had always liked honey, but these cookies were out of this world. I suppressed a moan. "These are delicious."

Harper winked at me. "Told you."

Claire was busy munching on a cookie, clearly loving it as much as Harper and me.

Francine stared at us, glad to see us enjoying her snacks. "So, what brings you here?"

Harper swallowed hard. "What makes you say that?"

Her grandmother narrowed her eyes at us. "Three beautiful, young women hanging around an old crone like me on a Sunday afternoon? I highly doubt it's just for the cookies."

"But, Grandma—"

Francine waved Harper off. "It's okay, dear. I'm just glad you came by, even if it's with a purpose."

Harper glanced at me.

I quickly finished eating my cookie and turned to Francine. "Actually, I was wondering if you could help me."

Francine frowned. "With what, my dear?"

"I told them you're a Wildthorn witch," Harper blurted out. She shrank in the couch, seemingly afraid of her grandmother's wrath.

But the old woman didn't lash out. She simply lost her smile as she stared at her with serious eyes. "It's okay. As long as you two keep quiet, it should be fine."

"You think the demon hunters would capture you if they found out?" Claire asked.

Francine nodded. "I know they would. I've seen it done before."

"It seems so wrong," Claire said, her voice low.

"Agreed, but since I live in a demon hunter town, there isn't much I can do about that." She glanced at me, her eyes softer than a moment ago. "How can I help you, my dear?"

"During one of my classes, I heard that Wildthorn witches can break almost any curse or bond." I lowered the neckline of my blouse, showing her the twin soul mark above my left breast. "Could you break a twin soul bond?"

Her brows pinched. "It's uncommon, because people who share a twin soul bond are destined to be together. They love each other." I suppressed a scoff, "But I think it could be broken."

I stiffened, my eyes going wide. "It can?" I had come to her, but deep down, I thought it would be impossible.

She nodded. "To be honest, I don't need to break it for you. With the right tools, you can perform the ritual yourself. That would be much more effective."

One more surprise. "And what do I need?"

"It's simple," Francine said. "You need a Wildthorn witch's wand, which is made from the wood of blackthorn trees. In front of a blackthorn tree, you use the wand to summon a curse-breaking demon called Tornar. You'll also need a few drops of your blood and of your soulmate's. The rest is simple."

Blood from my soulmate. Shit. "Can't I perform this ritual alone? Do I need my ..." I pressed my lips tight, not willing to say the word out loud. "Does the guy need to be with me?"

She nodded. "Yes. He has to perform the ritual with you."

Shit. I really wanted to leave him out of this. I wanted to do it and then go to him and say, "There, you're free of me. Be happy now."

"There's one little problem," Harper said. "Blackthorn trees are rare, and the only one we know of is right in the middle of the academy. How are you going to summon a demon there?"

"We can do it in the middle of night," Claire said. "Everyone will be sleeping."

"But what if the demon is a little loud?" Harper asked,

with a hint of sarcasm. All demons were loud, unless they were sneaking somewhere.

"How about a silencing spell?" Claire mused. "I saw a few of those in the spell books. Do you know any?"

Francine nodded. "I do. I can teach you to do that too, Erin."

Silencing spell, using a witch's wand, and summoning a demon? It didn't seem too easy. But this was for breaking the soul bond. It wouldn't be easy.

"Anything else I should know?" I asked, my resolution draining from my veins.

Francine held up a finger. She stood up and went to a bookshelf at the end of the room. There, she opened up the lower cabinet doors and picked up a thick leather book, and a long black box. Holding both items, she sat back down.

"Here." She handed me the box. "That's my wand. I'll let you borrow it for the ritual." Then, she pushed the heavy book at me. "And this is the spell book with the incantation you'll need." She scooted closer to me and opened the book on my lap. "This is the spell." She pointed to the page. "Tornar is a demon imprisoned by this spell. You'll summon him and he'll break the curse for you. But once that is done, you have to kill him."

"I'll have to battle a demon?" I asked, liking this entire spell a little less.

"He's strong, but he'll be contained by the spell," she explained. "Moreover, he's already dead, in a way. Killing him again is just the way to send him back to the realm he's imprisoned in."

"What happens if I can't kill him?" I asked.

"Don't worry about that," Francine said. "I'm sure you can kill him with a simple strike of your Dawnblade."

She went through the entire ritual with me, making sure I knew the order of each thing, and that I could pronounce the words I would have to chant.

After it seemed she was done teaching me the ritual elements, I frowned. "Aren't you curious why I want to break the soul bond?"

She entwined her long fingers together and rested them on her thighs. "I'm sure you have your reasons. You don't need to tell me. Besides, I'm not fully sure this will work. I think it will, but it's not guaranteed. However, if this ritual can't break the soul bond, nothing can."

I stared at the open page of the book. It seemed like a simple enough ritual, but with two special magics: the wand and a curse-breaking demon. "I'm sure it'll work," I whispered.

"Just a small warning," Francine said. "Once a curse or a bond is broken, there's no turning back. It can't be undone. So before doing this, be sure of your choice."

I closed the book and laid my hands flat against the cover. "I'm sure."

Was I? It wasn't as if I had a choice.

Up until now, I had been so caught up in the research, in the thrill of discovery. But had it been because I thought there was no way of undoing the bond? Now that the answer was literally in my hands, the thrill was gone, replaced by sorrow.

"Grandma, I had one of those dreams again," Harper said, fishing me out of my dark mind. "Can you interpret it?" She went on, telling Francine about what she had seen in her dream: a vast field with dark skies, hands rising from the ground, and dead birds flying toward her.

"It's an omen," Francine said. "Something bad will happen soon."

"To me?" Harper asked, her voice thin.

Francine shook her head. "Not necessarily. It could be to your school? To the entire demon hunter society."

The girls and I exchanged a significant glance. Yes, something bad would happen soon. A big war with King Brikan, and I was right in the center.

I frowned, confused. "You can interpret dreams?"

Francine looked at me. "It's one of my many talents. I can help decipher most dreams, find their meaning, and if they are more, I'll know that too." Her delicate brows dipped down. "Why? Do you have a dream you want interpreted?"

I cleared my throat. "It's more of a recurring nightmare, actually." I told her all about the nightmare with Brianne and Cindy, but I didn't tell her they were my half-sisters, and that King Brikan was our father.

"You never told me about that," Claire whispered, clearly disappointed with me.

"It's just … it felt too creepy and I was trying to forget it, instead of talking about it." Which was the truth. I hoped she believed me and wasn't mad at me. "But since we started talking about dreams …"

"You thought I could help you," Francine continued for me. She scooted to the edge of the couch. "All right. Give me your hands, my dear." Without hesitation, I placed my hands in her open ones. "Now, close your eyes and relax. Try to clear your mind."

With so much going on, clearing my mind was freaking hard, but I closed my eyes and tried anyway. I felt as Francine's power reached for me, and poked in my mind. I had never had anyone trying to enter my mind and I wasn't sure if I could stop it or not, but I tried relaxing some more and giving her free flow of all my thoughts, even if she ended up finding out things I wasn't willing to share with anyone.

I felt Francine's tension rippling for me.

A moment later, Francine stood up. "All right. That's not a nightmare. That's a spell in the form of a nightmare to bring you torment."

I blinked. "W-what?"

"Girls, help me here." Francine started pushing the coffee table away. We helped her out with that, and also with rolling the rug away.

A witch circle was drawn on the floor under the rug. "Sit down," she told me as she also took a spot on the floor, right in the center of the circle. She glanced at Harper and Claire. "You two might want to stand back a little."

"What's going on?" Claire asked, her tone fearful.

"I think a demon cast a spell to enter Erin's dreams, and show her something that would bring her agony."

"A demon?" Harper asked in a whisper.

I glanced to Claire. A demon? There was only one demon who could have done that to me. My dear father, the supreme demon, had been tormenting me for fun. My mother told me he liked playing games. So here was one more of his games.

Francine patted the spot on the floor in front of her. "I'll put a stop to that right now."

Still a little shocked, I sat down on the floor with Francine and gave her my hands again. "What now?"

"Just try to relax again," she said. "I'll do the rest."

I rolled my shoulders and closed my eyes. Despite trying to clear my head, the images surged up. The nightmare. Brianne and Cindy standing right here with me. Just the three of us in this living room.

"Help me," they asked, their voices a thin whisper.

My chest tightened. How I wished I could help.

I heard a low chant and looked around. There wasn't anyone else in here. But despite not being more than a whisper, the chant was strong.

I felt its magic wrapping around me. Expanding through the space. Reaching my half-sisters.

A crack appeared on the floor and bright light shone through.

I shot up and stepped back. "What the hell."

The crack grew and more light spilled through, bathing the entire room in a white daze. I covered my eyes as the light surrounded me.

I felt it pressing against me, making me breathless, then a tug and snap inside my mind, and a shock of pain that made me yelp.

Then it was all gone.

I opened my eyes, amazed that I was still seated on the floor with Francine, my hands in hers.

I gasped for air.

"Done," Francine announce, letting go of me. "I cut the link with whatever demon it was. The nightmares won't bother you anymore."

I pressed a hand to my chest, willing my heart to slow down. I felt like I had just run a marathon and I hadn't even moved an inch. "Thank you," I whispered. "Really, thank you."

Francine patted my knee. "Of course, my dear." She started getting up and Harper rushed forward to help her. "I just wonder, would you know which demon did this to you?"

I swallowed hard. "No, I don't know." After what she had done and her help with the bond breaking thing, I felt bad lying to her. I pushed to my feet. "But I'm glad it's gone now."

"Me too," she said with a warm smile.

The girls and I placed the rug and coffee table back in its place, then we sat back on the couch.

After some small talk about our classes and such, and more cookies, the girls and I decided to go. I held on to the book and the wand box and offered a small smile to Francine. "Thank you. I promise to take good care of these."

"No worries, my dear," she said, her tone dismissive. "I hope you know what you're doing."

Me too.

A moment later, Claire, Harper, and I were back in the car and driving to the academy. I was glad the girls hadn't asked me about the nightmare on the way back, or that they didn't stop me when we arrived and I ditched them, saying I had something to do.

I went to find Rey and tell him the news.

20

SATURDAYS AND SUNDAYS had been quiet. With no classes, and no training or research with Erin, I didn't have much to do, other than check on her every couple of hours.

But on Sunday, I lost track of her.

I had just seen her in her bedroom with Claire and Harper, and the next time I went to see her, she was gone. In my raven form, I flew around the entire campus, but there was no sign of Erin, Claire, or Harper.

Despair pressed against my chest, making it hard to breathe.

Where could Erin be? What was she doing?

I considered going to her mother, asking if she had seen Erin anywhere, or knew where Erin had gone. Martha would skin me alive for still keeping tabs on Erin, but right now, I wasn't worried about that. However, on my way to Martha's office, I realized I could check somewhere else.

As I thought, Claire's car was missing from the underground garage. Where the fuck were these girls?

I shifted back into my human form and went to the front

gates, where they must have drove by. Remi, one of the guards who had been under me when I was in charge of the campus security, saw me coming.

"Something wrong?" he asked, exiting the outpost beside the main gates.

"Claire Breevort left some time ago in her car," I said, my serious professor voice on. "Was she alone?"

"No, sir. She left about two hours ago with Harper Page and Erin Delman."

"Where were they headed to?" I asked, knowing all students who left had to inform the guards where they were going.

"To Chasseur Ville, sir," Remi said. "To visit Ms. Harper's grandmother."

My brows furrowed. To visit Harper's grandmother? Why? I nodded at Remi. "Thank you."

I walked along the main road, toward the Aster building, my mind reeling. They had never gone to Chasseur Ville like that before. Or anywhere else. Or was that just a lie? Visiting Harper's grandmother. That sounded like a lie.

But if it was, what the fuck were they doing?

My agony only increased with each passing minute. Erin was outside the gates with her friends, where demons could find her easily. That mark on her wrist didn't just announce to the world—or whoever knew how to read it—that she was King Brikan's daughter. It also attracted demons. It would be a miracle if she made it back in one piece.

I rubbed at my chest, trying to smooth the knots and pains there, as I paced around the underground garage. She had to come back soon. She had to.

Another hour passed, and nothing. I considered two things, I would either shift into raven and go after her, hoping she had told the truth and was in Chasseur Ville—because if she had gone someplace else, I would never be able to find her—or I would go to her mother and tell her Erin was missing. Martha was sure to do something, and as a mother, it would seem less desperate than a frantic guy going after his soulmate. The same woman he kept on rejecting.

I pressed my fingertips to my temple, sensing a fucking headache coming.

After another twenty minutes, I was done for. I shifted into my raven and—

Claire's car entered the garage and parked in its spot. I flew as high as the tall ceiling allowed me, and sat atop of one of the flat side of a lamp.

Holding a leather bound book and a black box, Erin disembarked the car. "Can you take this for me?" She handed the items to Claire.

"Sure," Claire said, taking the items from her. She frowned. "But ... where are you going? I thought we would organize everything we need now."

"I'm going to tell Rey," she said.

My heart skipped a beat.

She was coming to me?

Fuck.

Quietly, I flew out of the underground garage and then hovered over the courtyard for moment. Where was she coming to meet me? At my office? My classroom? My townhouse?

It was Sunday; she would come to my house.

I was fucking overthinking this.

Feeling like my blood was pumping too fast in my veins, I flew to my house and through the guest bedroom's window, which I always left a crack open for situations like this.

Inside my house, I shifted back and raced downstairs. I paced around the living room. Should I be seated? Eating something? Reading?

I halted.

The last time Erin had been here, she had ended up against the kitchen island, my hand under her blouse.

Under her bra.

A wave of heat coursed through me.

No, no, that couldn't happen again. I wouldn't let it. I was too fucking agitated with the prospect of her coming here, but I would act as always—I would ignore her, tell her I didn't want anything with her, then shut the door in her face.

And regret it forever.

I started pacing again.

Then the rap of a knock echoed from the front door.

Holding my breath, I went to it. I paused for five seconds, put on my indifference mask, then opened the door.

Erin raised her hands. "Before you kick me out or tell me you don't want to see me again, let me just tell you one thing."

My brows knotted. What the fuck was this about? "What?" I asked, forcing my voice to be taut.

"I found it," she said. Her golden eyes shone bright, but I couldn't figure out how she was right now. Sad? Excited? It was like she had learned to mask her emotions from me. "I told you that if I could break the soul bond, I would. So, let's do it."

I gaped at her. "Wait, what?"

"The soul bond. I found a way of breaking it. So now you can get rid of me for real."

I felt the urge to rub my ears, because what I was hearing couldn't be true. "But ... that's impossible."

Erin shook her head, her black hair spilling behind her

back. "No, it isn't. Well, it shouldn't be. We'll need to do a ritual with a witch's wand and some enchantment, but I already have everything we'll need."

"Slow down," I said, taking a step back. Erin didn't walk in. "You're saying we can break the soul bond."

"Yes, and we can do it tonight. The sooner, the better, right? The only hiccup is that we'll have to summon a curse-breaking demon to do it. But I think that between the two of us, plus Claire and Harper, we can control it."

"You're serious," I whispered.

Her delicate brows curled down. "Of course I am. You think I would joke about this? You think I would come to you to joke around?"

Holy fuck, she was serious. She had found a way of breaking the soul bond and she wanted to go through it right now.

But I didn't want to. Not really. In theory, life would be easier without the soul bond, but I didn't want it gone. It was the only thing, the last thing, that tied Erin to me. With that gone, then we had no reason to talk to each other. To see each other. To be around each other.

She would be free of me.

And I would be free of her.

My heart squeezed.

I didn't want that. But she couldn't know that. "All right. What do I have to do?"

Erin flinched, and her shoulders sagged a little. "The ritual has to be in front of the blackthorn tree, so we'll have to do it in the middle of the night. I'll come get you when everything is ready." Without another word, without another look, Erin took a step back, turned around, and walked away.

She left, completely unaware of the invisible knife she had plunged into my chest.

<hr>

AFTER MY SHOCK PASSED, I went for a walk. Perhaps I should have shifted and flown away, but my mind was too clouded for that.

Slowly, I made my way to the Lotus Lake at the edge of the academy estate. I sat down on a rock at the lake's bank, and breathed in. It was already October and the air was chilly, and getting colder every day. Short sleeves were gone, and jackets were needed at night. The leaves of the trees around the lake had already turned orange and red, and the flowers were gone for now.

I grabbed a pebble from the ground and threw it at the water. It skipped across the surface five times before sinking. I picked up another and weighed it in my open hand.

"What's the matter?" Harvey's voice reached my ears a moment before he stepped beside me, wearing shorts and a short-sleeved t-shirt. He had been running again. It was more than an exercise to him. It was a hobby. The guy liked running.

I shrugged. "Nothing."

"It doesn't seem like nothing." Harvey took off his shoes and socks and dipped his feet into the water, which was probably very cold.

I shook my head at him. "Don't worry. I can deal with it."

"Okay, man, whatever. Men don't share their feelings, right? Suit yourself." He turned his back to me and walked farther into the water, until it was covering his calves.

"First, get the fuck out of that freezing water before you

get sick, you idiot," I snapped. His body was probably hot and he was soaking in cold water. Was he stupid?

Harvey trudged to the lake's bank. "And second?"

I let out a long sigh. "Erin found a way to break the twin soul bond."

Harvey's eyes bugged. "You two share a twin soul bond? For real? That's so cool!"

"That is not cool," I protested. I needed him to be on my side on this. "Don't you see? This bond is tying us together, when she would be better off far from me."

"Do you hear yourself?" Harvey asked. "You love her. Why do you want to be far away from her?"

"Because!" Holy fuck, wouldn't anyone understand? "There are so many fucking reasons." Most of them were about threats to Erin's life by powerful men. I couldn't tell Harvey those reasons. And there was also her mother's warning to stay away from her. Going against the mother of the woman I loved wouldn't gain me any favors, would it?

Harvey poked his toe in the muddy earth. "All right, I won't argue with you. I guess you're old, and supposedly wise, and know what you're doing. If you say you can't be with her, then I believe you." He did? Whoa, I didn't expect to hear that. "Then breaking the soul bond is a good thing, right?"

"Yes," I whispered, trying to convince myself.

It was a good thing.

It was a fucking great thing.

Erin and I wouldn't have anything else binding us. She could walk away from me, and I could fly around her to make sure she was okay. She wouldn't even know I was there.

Simple.

"But just for the record," Harvey said, rescuing my mind from the ghetto it was in. "I think you're making a mistake. It's clear to me that you love Erin regardless of this soul bond. If you let her go, you're a fool." He turned to me, his eyes serious for once. "Don't go through with it. Don't break the bond. You two can find a way to be together despite all the opposition." He picked up his shoes and socks. "That's my opinion, at least."

He dipped his chin at me, then walked away.

The turmoil inside my chest only increased. I glanced at the blue sky and the setting sun. Soon, it would be dark and Erin would find me for the fucking ritual.

Was I ready for it?

21

ERIN

I WALKED from Rey's townhouse back to the dorms like a zombie.

What had I expected? That once I told him I had found a way of breaking the soul bond that he would give up on his facade? That he would hang on to me, beg me to not go through with it? That he would confess his love?

Thing was, as much as I hated to admit, I didn't think there was a facade. Before, I had my doubts that he was pretending to not like me, that he was pushing me away for whatever noble ideal he had in mind. But now ... now I was starting to think he really didn't like me.

But what about the times he had kissed me? Was that some pathetic guy thing? He couldn't resist a pretty girl who was willing to give him everything? Had he been playing with me? If it was, then he was an even bigger jerk than I first anticipated.

A headache started blooming in my skull, probably from thinking too much. There was nothing more to think.

Tonight, Rey and I would break the damn soul bond and he would be free of me, like he wanted.

Just like I wanted.

Right?

Claire and Harper were waiting for me in my bedroom, with the spell book and the wand over my desk. With a sigh, I sat down on my chair.

Harper leaned against the window. "Erin, I have to ask. Are you sure you want to go through with this? You heard my grandma. Once you do this, there's no going back."

"It's time they broke up," Claire said, sounding harsher than usual. "I mean, they were never together, but he keeps pulling and pushing her. It's annoying. I agree with Erin. It's time to end this. If he doesn't want to be with her, then they should erase all connections between them." Claire lowered her voice. "This is the only way she'll be able to move on."

"That is true," I said, "but I don't want to move on."

Claire frowned. "You don't?"

"By moving on, you mean finding some other guy to have a relationship with," I explained. "I don't want that. I don't want a relationship. Not now, not in a few years."

"But ..."

"It's okay," I continued, not letting Harper finish her barely formed sentence. "I have bigger things to worry about. *If* I survive my father, then I'll think about what comes next."

"You will survive your father," Claire blurted.

I snorted. "Yeah, because a half-demon like me stands a chance against the king of the underworld. Right." Tired of this subject, I stood up. "You know what? I'm hungry. Who wants to go to the cafeteria and have dinner with me?"

The girls didn't object and followed me downstairs. A bunch of students were eating, filling half of the tables and chairs. In a corner, some demon hunters talked shit to a couple of half-demons.

On another day, I would have gone there and joined the fight, and pushed those damn demon hunters away, but today … today I was too down to do anything. Even eat. I had lied about being hungry. I had wanted to do something instead of being holed up in my bedroom, wallowing in self-pity.

To make my day worse, I ended up behind Ava in the line to self-service.

Back to being a blond bitch, Ava turned around and snickered at me. "Hey, you. I feel irritated. I think that if I beat you up in a fight, I'll feel better."

I brushed past her. "Not today."

"Hey! For old time's sake! You know you like it when I hand your ass to you!" she shouted as I walked away, my tray practically empty.

I sat at my usual table and picked at my food. A moment later, Claire and Harper joined me, their plates full.

Claire frowned at my tray. "You said you were hungry."

I pushed the mashed potato and gravy with my fork—the only thing on my plate. "I think I lost it after bumping into Ava."

"Speaking of Ava, what's up with her? I thought she was becoming more friendly," Harper mused.

Claire shook her head vehemently. "More friendly? No. She hates us. Didn't you see that day when she yelled at us? That's her normal behavior."

"Hm, it's odd, then," Harper muttered. "I could have sworn she was warming up."

This wasn't the first time Harper had seen things not there. Before, she had also thought Rey really liked me. All illusions.

The two of them continued talking—about Ava, school, upcoming exams, the midterm games, whatever that was ... Meanwhile, I was lost in my numb mind, wishing this day could be over already.

I LAY in my bed in the dark, trying to sleep even if for only a few minutes, but I couldn't. Though my head felt like it had been stuffed with cotton balls, my body was uneasy, restless.

I tried counting sheep, to pass the time, but that only made me aware of how long I still had to wait.

After dinner, I retired to my bedroom. It seemed Claire and Harper wanted to get together and talk more, but I wasn't up for it. So I took a shower, put on a clean combat training uniform, and lay in bed.

All I was missing was the teasing tick-tock of a clock.

Then I would go nuts.

Finally, my phone rang with the alarm I had set—for two in the morning—and I jumped from my bed. My hands shook, my breathing didn't feel right, my legs wanted to run, but I forced myself to take a deep breath.

It was okay. It would be okay. This was for the best.

I put on a jacket over my clothes, grabbed the book and the wand, and sneaked down to the foyer. Three seconds later, Claire and Harper joined me.

"Ready?" Claire asked in a low voice.

I didn't answer. Instead, I jerked my chin toward the door. As silent as we could, we walked out of the building. Tiptoeing to the courtyard, we glanced side to side every few seconds, watching out for security guards who could be on patrol.

Thankfully, we didn't see any.

I looked to the sky. The moon was a tiny sliver in a dark canvas, and a few clouds covered the stars. Still, it was a beautiful night, only a bit too chilly for my taste. I tightened my jacket around me.

Under the tree, I set the book and the wand on the ground. "You think you can start the silencing spell without me?"

Claire nodded. "Sure."

"I'll be right back, then."

With my heart beating through my chest, I walked to Rey's house. I raised my hand to knock on the door, but it opened before I could touch it.

He stood there. Impassive. Stoic. Strong.

As handsome as ever in his dark combat clothes.

My heart broke more.

"Ready?"

Rey's brows knotted. "If you insist."

What did that mean?

I shook my head and walked away, not interested in any more gray areas. Between us, it would be only white and black from now on.

Rey followed me back to the courtyard. Under the blackthorn tree, he remained quiet while I helped Claire and Harper set up the silencing spell.

Then, I took the wand and uttered the words in the spell book.

A strong whoosh washed over us, the indication that the area around the courtyard had been sealed. Though this spell was called a silencing spell, it was much more than that. It also created a mirage around the designated area. If someone looked out from the Aster building, for example, they would see the normal courtyard. No students under the blackthorn tree. And if a guard walked around it, they wouldn't see or hear anything, unless they bumped into one of us.

This way, we could summon a demon and kill it without being afraid of getting caught.

"I think we can start," I said. "Claire, Harper, you two should stand back. Don't interfere unless you have to."

Claire nodded. "Only if Tornar is too hard to handle. Got it."

Both girls took several steps back, distancing themselves from Rey and me.

Then I faced Rey. My stomach tightened. I handed him the spell book. "Here. This is the chant." I spoke it out loud so he would know how to pronounce it correctly. "We'll repeat it while I start the ritual."

I turned from him.

"Erin ..."

I stilled, but didn't look back. "What?"

I heard his sharp inhale. "Nothing. Let's just get this over with."

What was left of my heart broke into a million pieces. Tears choked me, but I forced a long breath to calm down. I wouldn't cry in front of him.

I summoned my Dawnblade and started the ritual.

22

I couldn't believe I was going through with this. It was insane, right? And who said this ritual would work? Honestly, I was hoping it wouldn't.

Without much choice, I chanted the fucking words while Erin went around us, carving symbols on the patch of grass right in front of the tree with the tip of her Dawnblade. It was a witch's summoning circle.

Muttering the words with me, Erin came back and stood in front of me. She took the book, laid it on the ground, then picked up my hand in hers. She turned my palm up and looked into my eyes.

At that moment, when her bright golden eyes were locked on mine, when she was holding my hand, so close to me, I almost told her the truth—that I loved her and that I didn't want to break the soul bond.

But I swallowed those words and manned up. This was for the best. This was what her mother would have wanted for her, if she knew about the soul bond. This was the best for

Erin, no doubt. This way, she would have fewer things to worry about. This way, she would be in less danger.

Erin drew the tip of her Dawnblade across my palm, and a red line of blood appeared. Still chanting, she closed my hand into a fist. Understanding what I had to do, I squeezed my hand and the blood dripped onto the ground, right in the middle of the crude summoning circle.

Next, she repeated the process with her hand, her dark and thick blood mixing with mine on the ground.

I watched as she winced, probably in pain because of the shallow cut. An urge to take her hand in mine, to wrap something around it, even my jacket, hit me hard.

But I stood my ground.

My teeth gritted, I kept on chanting while Erin picked up the wand—a long, wooden stick with symbols carved along the tip—pointed it to the ground, and swirled it, drawing some symbols in the air.

A faint white light came from the summoning circle, and a tingling sensation crawled up my legs, the powerful magic pressing against me.

It was working. It was fucking working, and soon Erin would be free of me.

It was for the best.

It was for the best.

It was for the best, right?

The ground underneath my feet shook.

Erin and I took several steps back to steady ourselves as a dark cloud swirled in the middle of the circle, hovering a couple of feet from the ground.

"You can stop chanting now," Erin said, her wide eyes fixed on the cloud.

The cloud stretched, becoming long and slim. And then it

took shape. A male with milk-white skin, black symbols carved over his arms, pitch-black eyes, big bull-like hooves and horns. The demon stood in the middle of the circle as if it owned it.

From atop his seven plus foot height, the demon glanced down at us.

"What do you want?" Tornar asked, his voice grave.

"We want you to break the soul bond that connects us," Erin said without any hesitation.

Was this fucking easy for her?

Tornar glanced from her to me. "Hm, that's a powerful bond, but it shouldn't be a problem." The demon paused. "Just be warned. Once the bond is broken, there's no way to restore it."

"That's what we want," Erin said, her tone flat.

"As you wish." Tornar clasped his hands together.

The magic swirled around me. Desperation gripped my heart. No, no, I didn't want to do this.

I opened my mouth to stop this, to tell Erin we had to stop this, but before I could say anything, I felt it. A hand reaching inside my core, grabbing my soul.

And picking it apart.

I fell on my knees as the pain spread through my chest. Through my entire body.

"We need to kill him," Erin rasped. She too was on the ground like me, writhing in pain. "If we don't kill him, he'll escape."

Fighting through the pain, I extended my hand and tried summoning my Dawnblade, but nothing happened. I couldn't do it. I couldn't even keep my arm from shaking, or my head upright.

This was too fucking much.

"What if we can't?" I asked, my throat hurting with the effort to speak through the pain.

"I-I don't know." Erin groaned and curled into herself, her body shaking uncontrollably.

I wanted to reach for her, to smooth my hand down her back while the pain ran its course, but I couldn't even move an inch, much less comfort someone else while I was going through the same thing.

From the corner of my eyes, I saw as Tornar grew another foot or two and faced Harper and Claire. Both of them tried fighting him, containing him, but he was too much for them.

Harper summoned her Dawnblade and advanced on the demon. Trembling, Claire did the same, but she didn't look as confident with the sword in her hand as her friend.

Tornar sneered as he rammed into Harper and flung her several feet back. Even though she was shaking from head to toe, Claire tried standing her ground, but the moment the demon swatted at her, she crumpled to the ground.

That was it. The demon easily overpowered all of us.

He turned to us, a wicked grin in his wicked mouth. "Thank you."

Then he fled.

Tornar was now free to wreak havoc in the human world.

And it was all because of Erin and me.

I pushed up on my legs, but the pain shot like a shock to my limbs, and I ended up crumpling forward. Writhing on the ground, I gritted my teeth and tried enduring it.

It had to pass. This pain had to end at some point.

But instead of lessening, the pain only intensified.

The last thing I remember seeing before passing out was Claire kneeling beside Erin, crying for her friend.

23

I STARED at the ceiling above my bed, not seeing anything.

A knock came from the door, but I didn't answer it.

For a week now, I hadn't done anything but stared at the white, plain, and mostly flat ceiling.

The ritual had been successful, but all the rest hadn't worked well. We were supposed to kill Tornar after the ritual, mostly a symbolic death, as he was enchanted to go back to his supernatural prison, until someone else summoned him, used him to break something, then killed him so he could do it all again.

But we had failed that part.

To break the soul bond, Tornar had to rip a piece of our souls out—I learned that only after the ritual—and that hurt more than being stabbed in the heart. The demon took advantage of our suffering and inflicted more pain on us.

Then he escaped.

There was a freaking curse-breaking demon on the loose, and it was all my fault. I should do something about it, go after him, track him down, fight him, kill him ... but even thinking about that took too much of my energy. I didn't have the strength to get out of bed lately, or even raise a finger. I wouldn't be hunting demons any time soon.

After Tornar escaped, Rey and I fainted because of the pain. When I woke up the next day, I was in my bedroom—Claire and Harper had called Harvey to help out. I was told Harvey had gotten Rey to his house too, but I hadn't heard anything else about him since then.

I lowered the neckline of my blouse and glanced at my chest. The mark was gone. Erased as if it had been a henna tattoo. And a part of my soul had been taken away from me. Just a tiny bit, but enough to make me feel broken. In pieces. Incomplete.

I had been so sure that once the soul bond was gone that my feelings for Rey would disappear too. But that hadn't been true. To be honest, I thought I was even more in love with him now, since there was nothing connecting us, no fate that tied us together.

It was only our feelings.

My feelings.

But if Rey had rejected me before when we were connected, now he was probably indifferent to me.

And that ... that hurt most of all.

My bedroom door burst open and my mother stomped in. "All right, I'm done being patient." She slammed the door closed. "I was considerate for an entire week while you went through whatever this is." She wiggled her fingers at me, as if I had a contagious disease. "But enough is enough. You're going to tell me what is wrong, and we'll fix it."

I appreciated the sentiment, but there was nothing she could do for me. "I just want to be alone."

"Being alone and skipping classes won't help you graduate." She stood in front of me, her eyes impassive. "Whatever it is, you need to push through. You're stronger than this."

Shit, how I wished that was true. "Just … leave me alone."

"Erin," she snarled. My mother knelt down before me. "Listen to me. The midterm games start this weekend, and all third-year students have to participate."

"Midterm games?" I asked, confused. Something in the back of my mind sparked. I had heard about this. Third-year students didn't have normal midterm exams. They have some kind of physical games to go through, to show all they learned so far. "Oh, shit."

"Language!" my mother snapped.

"Oh, pardon me. Oh, poop," I said, provoking her.

She groaned, annoyed at me. "If you're done joking, then I suggest you get your ass off that chair and get ready. The games are supposed to be fun, but they can also be brutal. You need to be ready." She stood and smoothed out her suit. "Come on. You need to come to the arena and find out in which team you are on."

I stared at her. "What do you mean?"

"Students are assigned to teams of three. Go to the arena, check in, and find out who else is on your team." She offered me a small, knowing smile. "Pray they are as good as you are, because you'll need them to win."

AT FIRST, I thought about ignoring my mother's wishes. Who cared about midterms anyway? Did she think I cared if I failed all my classes?

Right now, I didn't care about anything.

But she didn't leave me alone. For the next three hours,

she either came to check on me and bug me, or she sent Claire, Harper, and even Harvey to check on me, and bug me in her stead.

Tired of them all buzzing in my ear, I got up and went to the arena with Claire.

A long, folding table was open to the side of the running track, with professors seated behind it, registering students as they checked in. I gave them my name, and they gave me a number.

Eight.

Claire showed me her number. Five. We were not on the same team. "Check there," she said, pointing to a wooden board a few feet from the improvised table.

I went to the board and checked the listing by the number.

"You've got to be kidding me," I muttered, staring at the names on the board.

My name was listed with Ava and Harvey.

"I'm not too happy about it either," Ava said, standing on my right.

"You two are badasses," Harvey commented as he appeared on my left. "I'm fine with that."

I rolled my eyes.

I turned around to face them, but the first thing I saw was Rey, standing several feet away, with a clipboard in his hands, talking to some students.

My heart squeezed.

I hadn't seen him since that night, since I thought we both would die because of the inexplicable pain we felt, because of what we had done.

And now here he was, looking as terrible as I felt, even though he too was pushing through it and doing what he had to. Did he look terrible because of the pain we had experienced?

I shook my head. It didn't matter. What was done was done. I had nothing linking me to him anymore. No bonds, no fate, no ties.

He was free, just as he wanted.

"What are you looking at?" Ava followed my gaze.

"She's staring at Rey," Harvey said, his voice tight. "We need to go talk to him for the orientation before the games begin."

Shit, Rey was working on these freaking games. And I had talk to him. This was already going downhill.

"You know what?" I said quickly. "I'm not feeling great. Why don't you two go to the orientation while I go lie down. I need to be rested for tomorrow, right? Later, you two can tell me all about it."

Harvey's eyes became two slits, as if he could see right through me, but I wouldn't change my mind. Even if I lost the first of the games because I hadn't gone to the orientation, I didn't care.

After a forced smile, I zipped away from the arena, leaving even Claire behind.

* * *

THE NEXT MORNING, all third-year students met outside the arena. We were given a special suit made of enchanted leather.

"These will protect you from being killed," Professor Genevieve explained. "But if you're hit, you'll be sore afterward."

Killed? These games were that intense? She went on to

explain about how the first game worked. Two teams would enter the arena and try to hit the opposite team members with a ball to get them out of the game, while dodging obstacles. Sounded like dodgeball on steroids.

It was so much more than that.

The students stayed on the bleachers on the side while the first two teams were taken to the arena and started the first round of the midterm games.

Claire, Peter, and Stella, against Harper, Ruby, and Justin, one of Tom's best friends. Professor Eleanor stood in the middle of the arena with them. She tossed a coin and indicated which team started with the ball.

Justin got the ball. The game started. He threw the ball at Claire, who barely moved an inch, taking her out of the match before it even started.

"Holy shit," I muttered, upset for Claire.

A minute after the beginning of the game, the obstacles finally showed up.

They weren't what I was expecting.

Tall walls rose from the ground around the arena, with dozens of holes. Then, long, thick wooden spears with metal tips shot out of the holes—appearing there as if by magic.

I gasped. What the hell?

The spears zipped across the arena fast and hard. The students had not only to dodge the ball, but also the spears.

Then one spear hit Ruby in the side and she went flying several feet. I held my breath as she lay flat on the ground, more spears zooming above her head. It seemed like a shudder had fallen over the bleachers, everyone waiting to see if Ruby was okay.

She was okay, right? The professors would have stopped the match if it was more serious.

Finally, she groaned and stood up.

These will protect you from being killed, I remembered Professor Genevieve's words about the uniforms we were wearing. Damn, she wasn't kidding.

Ruby tried to continue playing, but she was limping, and not long after another spear hit her in the chest, driving her to the ground again.

This was nuts.

Sick to my stomach, I turned around.

"Keep watching," Ava said from my right. "We need to make sure we understand the game. Perhaps there's a pattern to the whole thing. If we can figure it out, we'll win this whole thing."

"There's no pattern," Harvey said from my left, his voice tight. "It's just brutal."

That it was.

A couple more teams played. At least one member of each team limped out of the arena, incredibly hurt because of the spears. I gulped, knowing that was my fate too.

Then it was our turn.

Ava marched into the arena like a queen. She really seemed into this thing. Harvey didn't look happy to be here, just like me. But when our opposing team came in, I felt the blood in my veins warming up fast.

Tom, Gabe, one of his friends, and Olivia, a quiet girl.

All right. No matter what, now I refused to lose.

Because Harvey was on our team, Professor Eleanor was replaced with Professor Genevieve. She tossed the coin and gave the ball to us.

Harvey reached out for it, but Ava snatched it before he could. "This is mine," she said in a low voice.

Professor Genevieve retreated. She raised her hand high.

"Ready?" None of us answered, too focused on our adversaries. She lowered her hand fast. "Begin!"

With the force of an Amazon, Ava threw the ball to the other side of the court, taking out Olivia in less than two seconds. Tom picked up the ball and aimed at me. I was able to get out of the way, but then the shower of spears started.

While dodging the spears, Harvey got the ball and threw it at Gabe, but he moved because of a spear, and the ball missed him.

If we couldn't stop moving because of the ball, with the spears it was so much worse.

Tom grabbed the ball and bided his time. When Ava jumped away from a spear, he threw the ball at her, hitting her square in the chest.

Ava was out.

She left the court yelling colorful words at Tom, and even at Harvey and me. Apparently, she would kill us if we lost.

Harvey had the ball. He threw it at Gabe, but a spear hit him first, sending him skidding across the ground. He stayed down for a long time, making me even more agitated, just waiting to see if he was all right.

We had been warned these uniforms would save us from being killed, but right now, I wasn't really buying that.

I leaned forward as a spear flew behind me, whooshing an inch from my back.

This game was nuts.

Tom took the ball and threw it at me. I was so focused on the spears, I didn't pay attention to it, until Harvey pushed me out of the way. In the process, he was hit by a spear, right in his ribs.

He fell back on the ground, gasping for air.

Shit, he had saved me, but was hit really bad because of it. Guilt snaked through my chest.

I knelt beside him. "Are you okay?"

"I'll live." He groaned, clutching his middle. "Now, go win this game."

I pushed away the guilt and stood up.

It was Tom and me now.

From the other side of the court, Tom sneered at me. "This will be fun."

He threw the ball.

Just as two spears came in my direction.

Without much choice, I jumped and rolled on the ground.

My heart beat fast in my chest, when I stopped and glanced up. The spears hadn't hit me, neither had the ball. With a grin, I dodged the incoming spears and grabbed the ball.

Watching me, Tom lost the smile. He didn't stop moving because of the spears. Neither did I. But I knew that at some point, I would have a chance.

I ducked from a spear coming for my shoulder line. When I straightened, I saw Tom jumping forward, moving away from a spear.

I threw the ball.

It hit him square in the chest.

Instantly, the spears stopped.

"Team eight wins!" Professor Genevieve announced.

Ava ran into the court and jumped over me, tackling me into a bear hug. "You did it!"

I had to confess, I felt freaking awesome. After a week of feeling like I was on my death bed, I finally made a breakthrough. And it wasn't because I had won the game for my team.

It was because I had defeated Tom.

At least here, I wouldn't let him beat me up.

He glared at me from the other side of the court, and like a bitch, I winked at him.

24

REY

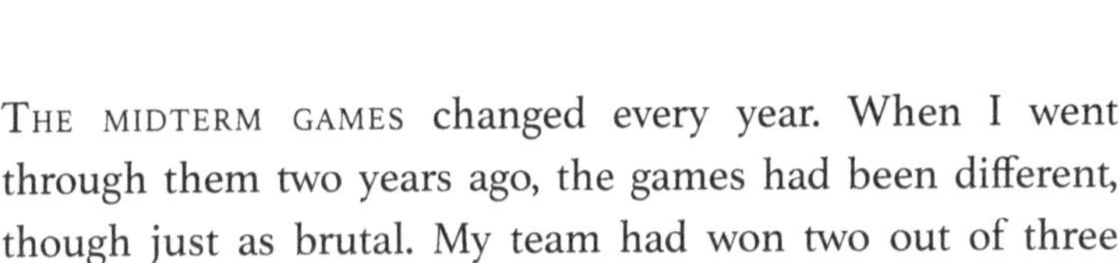

THE MIDTERM GAMES changed every year. When I went through them two years ago, the games had been different, though just as brutal. My team had won two out of three games, and we had the best grades of the entire third-year class.

This year, I was a professor, which meant I had to help out with the organization and running of the games. I had hoped I could excuse myself, but no excuse stuck.

It was pure torture to stand here, so close to Erin. Seeing her face off with Tom during the first game had been nerve-racking. Fuck, I hadn't seen Erin since we broke the bond over a week ago, but glancing at her was painful.

The fucking soul bond was gone, but not my feelings. I still wanted to be near, to check on her, to make sure she was safe. I still fought against myself to not get too close, to not go talk to her, to not confess my seemingly undying love.

I had thought, I had hoped, that once the soul bond dissolved, so would my feelings. I thought I was so obsessed about her because we were connected.

But that wasn't the case. I loved her, with or without a soul bond.

This past week had been torture. I had to put on a mask and continue my professor duties, while my soul ached. That was what I got for not speaking up, for not stopping the fucking ritual. Now Erin and I looked like walking zombies with a piece of our soul missing.

Breaking the soul bond had been a terrible mistake, in more ways than one.

Now Tornar, the curse-breaking demon, was on the loose. In my spare time, I had checked on Erin—she hadn't left her dorm room in an entire week, despite Claire's and Harper's insane efforts to cheer her up—and I flew around the area, searching for Tornar. I had even met other demons, trying to locate him, but to no avail.

It was like Tornar had disappeared.

If he resurfaced somewhere, killing innocents, I would never forgive myself.

The next morning, the third-year students got together around the arena, which had been changed during the night, for the next round. I seriously didn't want to be here, but because of my duties, I had been assigned to stand at the start line of the game, making sure the team on my side was ready. On the other side, Professor Genevieve stood with the other team.

It was a boring job, until it was Erin's turn.

She, Harvey, and Ava entered the arena and walked up to me. Erin looked everywhere, but never at me.

I cleared my throat. "You saw the other teams go, so you know the drill, right?"

Erin played with the strap of her armor. They were

wearing the same magical armor from yesterday, which protected them against killing blows. They would need it.

"Yeah, yeah," Ava said, sounding bored. "We know what to do."

"All right, then, take your positions," I told them.

Harvey shot me a glance and patted my shoulder. That night, he had helped Claire and Harper take Erin and me out of the courtyard. While Claire and Harper watched out for Erin, Harvey had stayed at my townhouse with me until I woke up. He had given me a sermon about how stupid I had been in breaking the soul bond and releasing a fucking demon.

As if I didn't know that.

"Easy," Harvey muttered, before walking away with Ava. They went through the side of the arena, and took their places, farther along the track.

"Are you ready?" I asked Erin. She looked up, straight ahead to the track in front of her, but she didn't answer me. I let out a long breath. "Erin, I'm asking as your professor. Are you ready?"

"Yes," she said, her voice harsh. It sliced through my chest.

Had her feelings gone away when we broke the soul bond? I hoped so. I hoped that the way she was ignoring me now was because she hated me, because she was disgusted by me. Wasn't that what I wanted from the beginning? I had tried being a jerk so she would take a hint and stay away from me. It hadn't worked then, but apparently, it had worked now.

Good. That was good.

Then why did it only make me hurt more?

"Here." I handed her the wooden baton she needed for this game.

Still not looking at me, she took the baton from me. Fuck, how I wanted her to say something. Anything. To yell at me.

I missed her, even when she was mad at me.

"Good luck," I whispered.

A short ring echoed through the arena.

Erin shot ahead, running as fast as she could, and I watched, my heart constricted in my chest.

This game was a speed relay. After running for several yards, Erin had to vault over a tall wall, which had been enchanted to melt or crumble once the students touched it, making it difficult to climb over it.

Erin slipped when the area around her hands started melting, but eventually, she made it across, a second before her opponent. At the end of that obstacle, Harvey was waiting for her. She passed the baton to him and he zoomed off.

He had to tuck the baton in a pocket and run while throwing daggers at dummy demons that showed up along the track. He had to hit at least seven out of ten, or his team would be disqualified. As usual, Harvey excelled at this kind of thing—he hit all ten dummies, gaining his team more points.

Next was Ava. She had to swim through a pool full of demonic fish that bit like piranhas. Her armor protected her from the worst, but when she exited the pool, she seemed tired, and her neck and ears were bleeding.

By then, Erin and Harvey had gone through the shortcuts and reached the end of Ava's course. She touched their hands, keeping the baton, and then three of them set off on the last part of the game: to run down a long, straight track. But there was a catch. Black thorns would shoot up from the ground and try to entwine around their legs.

Repaying Harvey's favor from the previous day, Erin

pushed Harvey to the side so he wasn't caught in the thorns, but two seconds later, more thorns jutted from the ground right in front of Erin. She tried jumping over them, but the thorns were too fast. They tied around her ankles and she fell to the ground with a loud smack.

My stomach dropped. I took half a step, in a desperate urge to go check on her. Holy fuck, this sucked.

Ava cursed, but went back to help Erin. The team would only be able to proceed to the last game if all members finished this one.

Even from a distance, it was clear Ava was yelling at Erin for being caught. They ripped the thorns from around Erin's ankles, and started running again.

They reached the finish line, but ten seconds after the opposing team. They would make it to the last game, but now points would be deducted from their total for coming in second.

After all teams had gone through and we disbanded for the day, I saw Erin walk away with Harvey and Ava. Claire tagged along with them since her team wasn't talking to her —she hadn't even tried to compete, and now her team was out of the game—but that meant she had to listen as Ava yelled at Erin and Harvey.

My hands twitched. I wanted to smack some sense into her. Couldn't she see that they were all limping, even bleeding? From grabbing the thorns, Erin's hands were bleeding too.

Fuck, how I wanted to go to her and do something.

Tired of all of this, I turned to the arena. Though I would rather go to my townhouse and rest for the rest of the day with a nice cold beer to help forget about the pain assaulting my core, I had to help set up everything for tomorrow.

I sat down at a desk and started going through each team's papers, reporting the right point numbers to them. A moment later, Crimson sat down beside me.

"You asked for a couple of weeks," he said, his voice low. "It has been a couple of weeks and nothing has happened."

I knew he would come after me at some point. But he was right. It was almost time. The full moon would be in three days. "Tomorrow," I told him. "After the final midterm game tomorrow. I'll reveal all I know about Randall, and you'll become the headmaster."

I just hoped I wasn't trading one evil dictator for another one.

I COULD ONLY GUESS that it was Randall and his inexplicable magic that changed the arena so fast in one single night. First, it had been the spears coming out of walls as if magic created and flung them out. Then, it had been the magic melting wall, and black thorns that sprouted from the ground.

Now, it was a huge maze with tall hedges.

The day was cold, the coldest we had so far, but the sun, already descending on the horizon, had shone bright. Now, with its orange and pink rays, it bathed the maze with golden light. The maze took over the arena's space and the bleachers, which had been moved back to allow for more space.

"The maze is filled with lesser demons," Professor Graham said, his voice tight. I knew he hated me, and if he could, he would execute me right here, right now. So he barely looked in my direction, and when he did, it was full of disgust. "You and your team have to defeat them, while advancing through the maze. Once you get to the end of the maze, wait there until a professor escorts you out. Once all teams have gone through the maze, we'll add the points and determine the winner. Right after, we'll announce everyone's grades in the midterm games. Is that clear?"

We all replied yes, and he let us walk to the maze's entrance. From there, the teams were allowed to enter the maze in intervals of fifteen minutes.

Finally, it was our turn.

"Fast," Ava snarled once we stepped through the hedges. Since these games started, she had been obsessed with winning. She had always been the blond bitch, but now she was the commanding blond bitch.

And there was a moment back there when I thought she could become my friend. But right then, I wanted the games done so I could get some distance from her.

The first set of demons we faced were screinors. "Don't let them scream," I said. I summoned my Dawnblade, sure no one would see it here in the middle of the maze, and slashed a screinor's throat as it opened its mouth to stun us.

One screinor screamed right in Ava's face. I plunged my sword in the demon's back. It stopped screaming, and Ava fell back, dazed.

Harvey helped her up. "Fight through it. Come on."

We continued down the maze. We took a few turns, which only irritated Ava, then we faced more demons: garrimps and muttmaugs.

"I thought Professor Graham said we would face lesser demons," I complained as we trudged on. We had been in there for over an hour and fought three sets of demons. My legs were starting to scream at me. "Some of these were neutral demons, not lesser."

"I know," Harvey said. He still held on to Ava. "I was thinking the same thing."

We kept going through the maze for another hour and

bumped into three more groups of demons—muttmaugs and garrimps again, and darkelths. Because of our enchanted armor, they couldn't really hurt us, unless they went for our heads, which weren't fully covered, but that didn't mean their strikes didn't hurt, or their magic didn't have an effect over us.

At some point, while we walked down a curved pathway, Ava glanced at me. "Care to explain how the hell you have that kind of Dawnblade?" I inhaled sharply. "Or do you think we are stupid and didn't notice?"

"I noticed," Harvey said, paying attention to the way ahead of us. "I just thought it would be rude to ask directly." He shot a glare at Ava before returning his gaze to the maze.

"It's not rude." Ava shrugged. "So, how did you get it?"

"The blackthorn tree gave me a piece of the blade," I told them.

Ava almost tripped on her own feet. "What?"

I explained how it all happened ... Rey and I had been looking for the gems during a treasure hunt. When looking near the tree, we noticed the piece of the magical wooden blade neatly imbued with the tree's trunk. Rey tried to get it, but couldn't. But when I tried, the tree easily gave it to me. Then, Rey helped me forge the sword.

The end.

I didn't tell them about our bonding moments while forging my Dawnblade, how we had imbued it with our magics, making it even more unique than it looked. That felt too intimate. Too raw.

Too hurtful.

"I think I see the end." Harvey pointed to what looked like an archway at the end of a long corridor. "I think that's it."

Glad to change subject and be done with this shit, I sighed in relief before we ran to the archway.

We stepped through and froze.

The end of the maze was actually the middle, where a bunch of pathways ended in a large round area, probably to confuse us more and throw us off course.

But that wasn't what made my blood chill.

Right in the middle of the clearing, Tornar stood, his long hands around the neck of a student. He squeezed until the student's neck broke, and then he flung the body of the student to the side, along with his dead teammates.

Somehow, Tornar had sneaked into the maze and had already killed three students.

"Oh my gosh," Ava breathed, her face paling.

The demon turned his pitch black eyes to me. "I was looking for you."

My stomach dropped. Why were all the demons looking for me? "I thought you had been smart and fled."

The demon stalked to us, showing off his razor-sharp teeth. I remembered Tornar was tall, but not this tall. He was at least three heads taller than us, and a lot wider. He was massive, and from what I knew, his magic was powerful too.

"You see, I can't really escape until I kill the people who last summoned me." His voice was scratchy and rough to my ears. "So I have to kill you and your boyfriend."

Tornar lunged at me.

Holy shit ...

I spun out of the way and stepped back, trying to push through the panic that pressed against my chest and thinking of a strategy. If only I had paid attention to Rey's classes ...

The demon turned around and groaned at me.

I summoned my Dawnblade. "Harvey, Ava, you'll have to help me."

My friends summoned their swords and stood by my side.

"Any tips?" Ava asked.

I shook my head. "I have never heard of this kind of demon before. I have no idea what it can do."

"One way to find out." Harvey twirled his sword in his hand and charged the demon.

I gasped as Tornar leaned back, avoiding Harvey's blade, but then advanced fast, wrapping his hand around Harvey's neck. He pulled up, until Harvey's feet were off the ground.

"No!" Ava screamed before running at the demon. To Tornar, she was nothing but a fly. As she got close to him, the demon slapped her side with his big claws, pushing her aside and out of the way.

Ava landed across the maze, her fall broken by the hedges.

No, this demon wouldn't defeat us. He couldn't.

I lowered my sword and took a few steps closer. "Tornar." The demon looked at me. "It's me you want. Let him go."

His black eyes twinkled and I held my breath, afraid he would do the same thing he did to that other student, to Harvey, but finally, he tossed Harvey away as if my friend was a crumpled piece of paper.

"Let's play," the demon hissed.

I didn't dare take my eyes off the demon to check on Harvey. I would believe he was all right. I tightened my grip around the hilt of my sword. "It's just you and me now."

Tornar's lips curled into a wicked smile. "And what's the fun in that?"

The demon threw his claws forward and magic gushed out of them. A strong, bright magic raced toward me. I stepped back, but I wasn't fast enough for it. I wasn't strong enough.

The magic, deceivingly white, encased me, pushing

against my body as if I was immersed in deep water. My chest screamed, my throat closed, my head felt like it would implode. I gasped for air, but there was only magic. Tornar's hostile magic. It suffocated me.

My Dawnblade disappeared from my hands as I tried to claw through this intangible magic. "C-coward," I croaked.

"Me, a coward?" Tornar asked, his rough voice full of sarcasm. "Why is a demon a coward when he plays with all the cards that were dealt to him?"

Then he turned from me.

And stalked to my friends.

I panted, trying to scream, to say something, to persuade the demon to focus on me. Only me.

On the other side of the maze's center, Ava helped Harvey to his feet. Both looked like they couldn't take one more step before falling face-first and never getting up again.

If they faced Tornar in this condition, they would be killed.

I racked my fuzzy brain, fighting for my next breath as much as I battled for a next thought, a new idea. Something, anything that would help my friends. Help me.

My eyes scanned the area, but all I saw was the vast green maze's center and the bodies of at least a dozen students who had arrived at the center before us.

Bodies.

My stomach twisted with the idea that came to mind, but I was running out of time.

Opening my mouth and trying to inhale some air, I summoned my power. I called my magic—the dark one. Like my mother had taught me, I sent my magic to them and chanted the demonic words of the spell.

At first, nothing happened and I thought I had done it wrong. Or that I didn't have the power necessary to do this.

But then, they moved. First their fingers, then their arms and heads. When I ordered them to stand up, they did. When I ordered them to march to Tornar and summon their Dawnblades, they did.

My head swam; my vision darkened. This magic around me was too damn powerful. Through my thoughts, I ordered the dead bodies to attack fast.

A moment later, the magic was gone and I fell to my knees on the ground, gasping for air and coughing. Forcing myself to get past it, I blinked and looked ahead. Right in the middle of the maze's opening, Tornar fought with the dead bodies. He cut through them like they were plastic straws, but since they were already dead, they kept on going, they kept on attacking.

Behind them, Ava and Harvey stood with their swords in their trembling hands. Eyes wide, they watched the scene.

I swear, I felt the same, but there was only so much I could do right now.

Pushing through the numbness and pain assaulting every cell of my body, I stood up and summoned my Dawnblade. After taking a deep breath, I ran to Tornar, who was busy fighting twelve dead bodies and didn't see me coming.

When I was right behind him, I said, "Look here, you ugly thing."

The demon turned.

And I pierced my sword into its chest.

Tornar's dark eyes widened. "No!" he croaked as the magic in my sword spread through his body. His white skin turned gray and his eyes dulled.

I pulled out my blade and his body fell at my feet.

"What's going on here?"

I made my Dawnblade disappear before anyone saw it, and released the magic holding the dead bodies. They crumpled to the ground, like paper, all around Tornar's dried carcass. Then I turned to the new voice.

It was Professor Graham. He was in front of all other professors and school board members, including my mother and Rey. Both of them had similar looks on their faces—jaw set, and eyes wide, with a glint of desperation and fear in them.

Ava and Harvey stood by my side, their Dawnblades still in their hands.

"It was a higher demon, professor," Harvey said. "It killed the students and attacked us."

"No, not that." Professor Graham faced me. "What have you done with them?" He pointed to the bodies of the students a few feet from me.

"It was necromancy," Professor Wesley said. "I've seen it before. Erin used necromancy to reanimate the bodies of the fallen students."

Professor Genevieve gasped. "That's the darkest of magic. Completely forbidden."

"Is that true, Erin?" Professor Graham asked. "Did you use necromancy just now?"

Shit. I gulped and answered, "Yes."

The professors gasped. They turned to each other, and I heard words like "forbidden" again, and also "expelled."

That was it. I had been saved from being expelled way too many times. There was no way I could be saved now.

Professor Graham pointed at me. "Erin Delman, you committed a grave sin inside this academy. That shall not be forgiven. You'll be ex—"

"It's my fault," my mother shouted, coming forward. She stood between Professor Graham and me. "It was my idea. Erin didn't want anything to do with it. I taught her how to do necromancy."

"Martha," Professor Genevieve uttered. "You did what?"

"What the hell are you doing?" I asked her in a low voice. There was no way I would be forgiven for this, and now she was getting herself into this mess unnecessarily.

"In fact, Erin had never attempted it during my lessons, because she didn't agree with it," my mother said, probably hoping she could sway the school board that it wasn't really my fault. "When facing this higher demon, she might have felt she had no other choice. If she hadn't used necromancy, Ava and Harvey would be dead now."

Professor Eleanor's eyes bulged as she stared at her son. "Is that true?"

Harvey nodded. "If she hadn't done that, we would be dead right now."

"It's true," Ava added, a high pitch to her voice. "She saved our lives."

"That doesn't change the fact that Erin used forbidden magic on school grounds," Professor Graham insisted, his face turning red.

"But she saved her team members." The professors quieted down as the headmaster walked into the maze's center, followed by a handful of guards. Standing tall, the headmaster turned to me. "It took guts to perform such horrible magic to save your friends."

Professor Graham pointed his finger at the headmaster. "What? Are you siding with her?"

"I think we can agree on giving Erin a punishment for using dark magic, but other than that, she killed a higher demon and saved her friends," the headmaster said. A nervous pressure pushed against my chest. How many times would he save me from being expelled or killed? "Erin will remain at the academy."

Protests rose from all the professors, except from my mother and Rey.

"That isn't right!" Professor Graham shouted. "Professor Martha is also at fault here. How can a professor of this esteemed academy teach something so dark to a student?"

The voice of the others joined his, all asking for a punishment for my mother too.

The headmaster glanced at my mother, seemingly bored. "All right. Erin Delman will stay, but Martha Belmont will be fired as of this moment." He threw out his hands. "Guards, escort her out of the school."

"What?" I asked, advancing to my mother. "That's unfair."

"Stay quiet," my mother snapped, her voice low. "It's fine. I'm okay. Just stay here."

The guards halted beside her. One of the guards, Tavin, held his weapon, not pointing it at my mother, but letting her know it was there. "This way." He gestured to one of the maze's corridors.

My mother gave me one last supplicant glance, then went with them. But two steps later, she paused and turned to Rey. "Forget what I told you. Just … just protect her."

What the hell was she talking about? I stared from her to Rey and saw as he dipped his chin at her.

The guards pushed my mother, and she started walking again, until she disappeared inside the maze with them. I wanted to go after her, but Ava must have sensed my turmoil as she grabbed my arm and kept me by her side.

"Just stay quiet or you'll make things worse," she whispered to me.

The headmaster faced the professors. "Now that that's resolved, I'll let you take care of the student's bodies."

I glanced around, realizing there were more people in the center of the maze than a minute ago. The third-year students and the half-demon army spilled from several maze corridors, forming a big circle around all of us. Among them, I spotted Claire and Harper.

Shit. Had they seen all of this? Did everyone know what I could do now?

The thought of reanimating dead bodies disgusted me, and actually doing it was even worse. I could only imagine how the others felt about it.

Professor Crimson stepped forward. "It's time."

The headmaster frowned. "Time for what?"

The buzz of cell phones vibrating started low, but then some phones hadn't been put on silent, and they rang through the maze. Several professors and students picked up the phones hidden in their pockets.

I knew some of the students carried them all the time despite being forbidden, but I didn't think it was this many.

Everyone stared at the screen in their hands, their eyes huge.

"What is going on?" I asked, confused. Without a phone of our own, Harvey, Ava, and I approached the nearest student—Peter. He extended his arm so we could look at it.

Instantly, my stomach dropped.

I wasn't ready for what I saw.

The video came through just as I had programmed it.

Earlier in the day, before the last midterm game, I had sneaked into the main office in the Aster building and hacked into the school system. I uploaded the video and programmed it to be sent to everyone's cell phones as a message or an email at a certain time. I was sure a lot of the staff, professors, and students carried their phones with them, even though it was forbidden.

Now, all of these people were having a look at the terrible ritual Randall performed every full moon.

My phone pinged too, but I ignored it, not wanting to see the fucking ritual again.

"What's the meaning of this?" Professor Genevieve asked, holding on to her phone for dear life.

Professor Graham stared at Randall with big, incredulous eyes. "Randall, is this true?"

Randall lifted his chin, looking down at us as if we were mere bugs in his path. "What are you talking about?"

Professor Graham snatched Professor Astrid's phone from

her hands and approached him, showing him the video.

Randall inhaled a sharp breath, but didn't seem bothered or nervous. Quite the contrary. Randall always had a regal air about him, with his tall figure and set posture, but now he squared his shoulders even more, looking like a fucking god.

For a moment, I though he wouldn't say anything, or deny it all. Instead, he said, "Yes, it's true. I kill useless demons, worthless humans, and powerful witches, and absorb their powers."

"You ... you drink their blood," Professor Eleanor said, her face pale.

Randall shrugged. "That too."

"Why?" Professor Adeline asked, her voice faint.

"Simple. The ritual gives me immense power and immortality. That's how I've been alive for so long. That's how I'm so powerful, not even higher demons dare come after me."

"That's wrong," Professor Graham spat.

Ignoring him, Randall turned in a circle, looking at everyone around him. "Demon hunters could become the most powerful beings in the world, if you allow yourselves to be." He extended his hand. "Join me in creating a brand-new world where demon hunters and half-demons are at the top of the food chain."

Professor Crimson gasped. "You mean, you want us to do the same ritual as you do? You have gone mad!"

"Mad, perhaps, but oh, so very powerful," Randall said with the hint of a smile.

"We can't condone this," Professor Astrid said.

Professor Wesley nodded. "Astrid is right. We're better than this."

"Lock him up!" someone shouted from the back. A student, no doubt.

"Kill him!" another one yelled.

People were growing agitated, cries of fear and rage rose from the crowd, and the professors stood in front of Randall, like a barrier.

"Guards," Professor Crimson said, his tone loud and hard. He pointed to Randall. "Arrest him!"

The guards hesitated, but when Remi finally aimed his weapon at Randall, all the others followed suit.

Loud laughter bubbled out of Randall's mouth. "You think you can stop me?"

This wasn't going like I pictured at all. Randall was too fucking powerful, and he could take most of us down with a simple blink of his eyes.

Remi took a step forward. "Don't make me use force."

Randall laughed more. Then his laugh was gone, and he snickered at Remi before flicking his wrist.

Remi and all the guards went flying several feet back. Some smacked right into the students, knocking them down.

Dawnblades appeared in the professors' hands. Following their lead, I summoned mine too. I gripped the hilt tight, a little eager for a fight against Randall. I knew I could never win, but I would do my best to give him some trouble.

"Stand down, Randall," Professor Graham shouted. "Stand down before we kill you."

"Kill me?" Randall called his sword, the first Dawnblade. In the blink of an eye, Randall spun around and swiped his sword wide, slashing across Professor Graham's throat.

Blood spluttered out as Professor Graham dropped his sword and clutched his neck. Professor Genevieve and Astrid knelt beside him, while Professor Wesley, Eleanor, and the others raised their swords at Randall.

The students and other staff around us gasped and whimpered, shocked by the twists this night was presenting. A few feet to my side, Erin took a large step back with Harvey and Ava. Harper and Claire were right behind them, also as pale and shocked as the rest.

"Don't you get it? You can't kill me." Randall twirled his sword in his hand. I knew he wouldn't go down easy, but I was starting to think this would be much, much worse than I first imagined. He smiled at the terrified faces of the students around the place. "Who else will stand in my way?"

Practically limping, Remi and the other guards returned to their positions. "We will," Remi said. Though his hand shook, his voice was unwavering.

"So be it." Randall's blade disappeared and he raised his hands. Vines full of thorns sprouted from the ground, much like the ones from the games yesterday, and wrapped around the guards.

Remi and the others squirmed, but that only made the vines tighten around them, prickling them with their thorns.

"Randall, stop this!" Professor Genevieve shouted. "You've already been unmasked, and we won't follow you even if you kill us all. But without any demon hunters on your side, you won't have a society to fight for. To rule. You need us."

"Just surrender!" Professor Crimson said. By now, he probably noticed things would be harder than planned.

"I won't have a society?" Randall tsked. "Let me rectify that."

He snapped his fingers.

Gasps echoed from the crowd.

What the fuck was happening?

Then, I saw it.

Standing with her friends, Erin's eyes rounded as the necklace around her neck glowed.

27

ERIN

THE PENDANT around my neck shone bright.

Not just mine. All of the half-demons had the same amulet as I did, and they all glowed like mine. The light was visible in the crowd, like fireflies in the dark.

"What's going on?" Claire asked, staring at me.

"I-I don't know," I muttered, feeling the pendant tingling against me.

A jolt like a shock traveled from the amulet into me, filling my chest with a brutal, dark force. I fought against the foreign power, but it was too much for me.

In the center of the maze, Randall lifted both of his hands high. "Now, Black Knight Army, rise!"

My body straightened, my head jerked forward, and my legs took steps I didn't order them to.

Desperation gripped me.

"I can't control myself," I told my friends.

"It isn't only you," Harvey observed, his eyes scanning the area.

All the half-demons seemed to be in a daze, walking

toward Randall.

"Attack!" Randall shouted.

Just like that, my Dawnblade appeared in my hand and I turned on my friends. "Guys ... I can't control it!" I lunged at them.

Harvey pushed Ava out of the way, and Harper twisted around with Claire. I spun around and went for them again, my movements precise, my sword, the one I couldn't reveal yet, swinging side to side.

Ava drew her sword and parried one of my strikes. "Stop this!"

"I can't." I tried glancing around, but my head didn't obey my orders. "I think all the half-demons are being controlled by Randall." Another jolt of dark power hit me, like a wave rolling inside my body. I bent forward, gasping for air. It was much stronger than me and it was taking over. I wouldn't be able to hold on to my own thoughts much longer. "You guys have to knock me out."

"We won't hit you," Claire snapped.

Claire.

My best friend.

The weakest of them all.

The dark force pushed, and I lunged at her.

With a yelp, Claire lifted her arm to defend herself. My sword slashed across her skin.

Blood dripped from her arm to the ground.

"Holy shit, Claire," I croaked, fighting against the foreign power, but unable to do anything. "I can't do this. Please, knock me out!"

With wide, fearful eyes, Claire stepped back, and Harvey blocked me from her. "I don't want to hurt you."

"You have to," I told him, practically begging. "Please."

Then another person appeared beside Harvey. "Then fight me," Rey said. His eyes fixed on mine, he twirled his sword.

I tried shaking my head, but I couldn't even do that. "I can't control it. I don't want to fight you, but I have to."

"It's okay. I've got you." Rey beckoned me forward. "Fight me and only me. You'll be distracted and won't hurt anyone else."

"I don't want to hurt you," I whispered, fighting against the will to jump over him and pummel him. The darkness spread some more.

"You won't." His voice was serene. Calm.

Unable to resist it anymore, I advanced on him. An expert fighter, Rey parried my strikes, one by one. More than that, he knew how I fought and he knew the way I would attack.

He could hold me back, even if for a little while.

But the darkness pressed inside me, demanding more of my senses, more of me. Soon, I would be a robot, striking down anyone in front of me.

I brought my sword down, aiming for his head. Rey twisted out of the way and posed himself, waiting for my next attack.

"Whatever this is, it's going to take over, Rey," I told him. Though I couldn't see much since I couldn't control my head, I took a good glance around every time I had to turn. It was pure chaos around us with all the half-demons fighting the demon hunters like mindless monsters. I had seen bodies on the ground, even though I couldn't see faces. It was a massacre. "Please, knock me out."

A line appeared on Rey's forehead. "I have a better idea." He twisted his Dawnblade with mine, making me lose the grip around my sword. My sword fell on the ground with a thud. Then he stepped right into me and closed his hand over the amulet. He closed his eyes and poured his magic into it. Though he was a half-demon like me, Rey's magic wasn't nearly as dark as Randall's, but since his connection was strong because he was holding the amulet, his power chased the darkness away.

The pendant cracked and the magic fled from my body. My knees trembled. I went down with a gasp, but before I could hit the ground, Rey wound his arm around my waist and pulled me to him.

"Are you okay?"

His eyes, almost silver now, locked on mine. His mouth so close to mine. His warm, powerful body pressed to mine.

He had saved me.

Again.

"Yes," I breathed out. "Thanks to you." If I could, I would have lingered in his arms for a moment longer, but I couldn't. Clearing my throat, I stepped back and pulled the amulet over my head. "What did you do?"

"Just fought the residual magic inside the amulet with my own," he explained. "My guess is that we can do the same with all the half-demons."

I looked around. The Black Knight army was out of control. "Let's do it."

Rey and I ran to the nearest half-demons. We had to fight our way to get close to them and be able to grab the pendant. I did as Rey explained, though at the first moment, the darkness pushed back and I almost lost. But after that, I knew what to expect. I went around, grabbing pendants, fighting the darkness, freeing one half-demon after another from Randall's control, and telling them how to do the same.

Soon, the half-demons who were still alive joined the demon hunters, and we all turned against Randall.

"It's over, Randall," Professor Crimson said. "Surrender now!"

"Never!" Randall spun around and ran out of the maze.

What the hell?

We all went after him.

28

REY

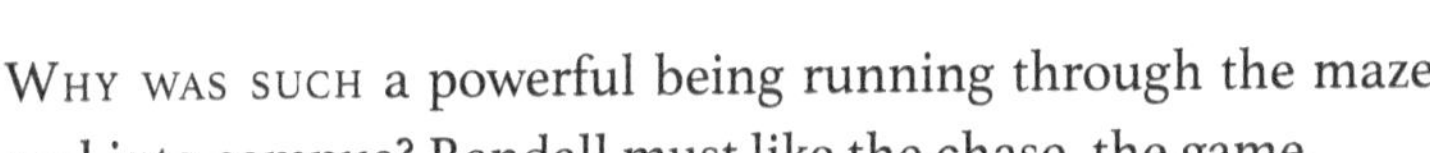

WHY WAS SUCH a powerful being running through the maze and into campus? Randall must like the chase, the game.

But he attacked every time someone got close. Besides leaving a trail of bodies as we raced after him, Randall sent his magic to the top of the buildings like lightning. It hit the corners, and stone and concrete fell, shaking the ground, making us lose balance. Sometimes, the rubble landed on top of people. Then, as if that wasn't enough, Randall sent fire to the buildings and vegetation on our way, making it all burn.

He ran toward the courtyard. I had a feeling that if he crossed into the Aster building, he would disappear. He would flee and we wouldn't ever find him again, unless he came to us.

I couldn't let that happen.

Using my half-demon magic, I increased my speed—but not a lot. I didn't want anyone to think I was half-vampire and put me through something worse. I outran everyone else and caught up with him right in front of the Aster building.

Sensing me, Randall turned to me, his arm outstretched. An invisible hand closed around my neck and lifted me up. "It was you, wasn't it?" He shook his head. "After all the trust I put in you, all we went through together, you betray me like that?"

"Trust?" I gasped against the force pressing against my windpipe. "I knew you never trusted me, and you knew I never really trusted you."

Randall shrugged. "See? We were the perfect pair." His magic squeezed my neck some more. Black spots clouded my sight. This had been fucking stupid. Did I really think I could fight against the first demon hunter?

"Drop him!" Erin shouted from somewhere behind me.

My stomach dropped. Erin? Here? No, no, no.

Randall's laughter echoed through the courtyard. "What are you going to do if I don't?"

"This."

At first, I couldn't see what Erin was doing, but then they showed up in front of me—her zombie figures. They all ran at Randall. Dozens of them. With visible thirst, they attacked the headmaster headfirst.

The magic around my throat loosened, and I fell on the ground, breathing hard. Without time to waste, I pushed up and turned to her. Erin stood a few feet behind me, her hands stretched to her sides as she controlled the many zombies. They were just as powerful as she was, and even though Randall was cutting through them like water, they were too many, and Erin kept conjuring more and more.

I could see the spell was draining her fast.

I glanced behind her. Finally, the others were catching up to us. Professors Genevieve and Eleanor took the lead. They ran past Erin and me, and charged Randall. Erin withdrew her zombies enough so they could sneak in.

Genevieve and Eleanor teamed up and took Randall by surprise. When Eleanor landed a beautiful back wheel kick to Randall's shoulder, making him lose balance, Genevieve came from behind and took his Dawnblade from him.

Enraged, Randall turned to her.

Using his Dawnblade, Professor Genevieve pierced Randall's chest.

He folded to the ground.

The Dawnblade, buried deep into his chest, shimmered. Orange freckles appeared from within and soon, the sword burned from inside out, turning into dust.

And Randall drew his last breath.

Finally, Erin let go of the zombies.

Breathing hard, she fell to her knees. I rushed to her. "Hey, are you okay?"

She inhaled deeply and nodded. "Just … that was a lot."

I held on to her upper arms, afraid she would pass out on me. "But we did it. We caught Randall." I glanced to where his body was on the ground, surrounded by the other professors. "Randall is dead."

Erin stared at his body for a moment. "Is he really gone?"

I pondered. Such a powerful being. Fighting us all a few seconds ago, and now immobile on the cold stone ground. Seemed unlikely. But … "He was stabbed with his own sword. I think the one thing that could really kill him was his own Dawnblade."

She nodded slightly. "I guess so."

"Don't worry. We did the right thing. He was pure evil, and now he's gone."

Letting me help her, Erin stood up. She turned back and scanned the place. The fire was spreading fast, and the Hyacinth and the Iris building were practically rubble. Bodies littered the pathways between the destroyed buildings.

"But we lost so much," she whispered.

29

THE BATTLE HAD ENDED, Randall was killed, his body instantly burned to make sure he really was gone, but the chaos continued.

The fire was put out, the buildings that were breaking down were cordoned off, and the courtyard was off limits. The fire had raged through it, burning everything but the blackthorn tree. The magical tree didn't seem one bit affected by anything that went on.

Soon after it all happened, the demon hunters had come down from their outpost in the mountains and took control over the situation. Among them were Hadrian, Harvey's father; Alain, Ava's father; Andre; Doreen; and Norah.

I hadn't had much contact with Norah, but she came to check on me, ask me if I was all right. For some reason, I liked her. Maybe because she had helped us with Farrah, showing me she was different from the other demon hunters. She didn't see the world in black and white, and I appreciated that.

After all the bodies were picked up and the surviving students were accounted for, students, professors, staff, and demon hunters got together outside the academy walls for a funeral. We had lost so many people, including Professor Graham and Adeline, guard Remi, and students—like Peter and Ruby.

Ava and Harvey were distraught over the loss of their friends. I wanted to stand by them and comfort them, but with their parents there, who were anti-half-demon to the core, I didn't dare get too close. But I couldn't approach Claire either. When I tried to apologize for hurting her, she seemed ready to bolt. I could see it in her eyes—she was afraid of me. The bandage on her arm was a reminder that I had lost control and attacked her. I couldn't blame her if she never spoke to me again.

But that only made the hole inside my chest bigger.

Because Randall was gone, the school board got together for a quick meeting and appointed Professor Crimson as the new headmaster. He looked pleased with himself, as if he had planned all of this, just to secure this position.

But that was insane, wasn't it?

During this meeting, they discussed the future of the half-demons and the Black Knight army. Apparently, the school board acknowledged Randall had controlled them against their will, and they would be given another chance, even if a lot of professors and full-fledged demon hunters were firmly against it. Next semester, the half-demons could return to the academy.

After all that, the students were dismissed from school. We were only halfway through the semester, but with half of the school destroyed, it wasn't like we could have classes and live normally here. Plus, reconstruction would be faster if no one was around.

I talked to my mother on the phone for a few minutes while I packed my bags in my bedroom. Most of the students were already gone, but I was trying to stay out of sight for a while. If they were all afraid of me before, if they hated me before, now with the news that I could use dark magic and practice necromancy spreading through the academy, it would be even worse.

Another thing that was bothering me nonstop was the fact that some people certainly saw me fighting with my Dawnblade. Though it hadn't been brought up yet, I was sure a lot of people had noticed my sword was different from theirs. I was afraid to consider what would be done about that.

But for now, I focused on the plan my mother and I had hatched. She was on her way back to the academy to pick me up. We would rent an apartment in a random town close by and hide for the time being.

I wasn't eager to live with her again, but I was counting the seconds to leave this place. Until recently, it had felt like home.

Now, I wasn't so sure.

I shoved my last shirt inside my duffel bag and zipped it up as a knock came from my bedroom door. I stilled, hoping that whoever was it thought I was already gone and left me alone.

"Erin, I know you're in there."

I sucked in a sharp breath. What was Rey doing here? Maybe he was bluffing, just testing me, thinking I was here. I tried my first plan: to stay quiet so he would leave.

"Erin, please."

Shit.

Bracing myself, I opened the door.

Yeah, no matter how many times I prepared myself, the sight of him always wreaked havoc inside me. It had been almost thirty-six hours since Tornar's attack and everything else that ensued after. He had cleaned up and put on dark jeans and a black sweater. His hair was still damp and combed back, showing off the sharp angles of his handsome face.

I wanted to tell myself that I would have used my magic to run faster and fought Randall for anyone, but I wasn't so sure. Probably for Claire and Harper, maybe for Harvey and Ava ... but I would be lying to myself.

I had seen him zipping past everyone, gunning for Randall with all he had. Knowing exactly how he was running so fast, I did the same and reached him in time to save him.

If I hadn't done that, if I hadn't gotten there in time ... I didn't want to think about it.

In need of a shield, I crossed my arms. "What is it?"

Rey ran a hand through his hair. "Can we talk?"

"We're talking."

He groaned. "Please, Erin."

What else could he want to talk about? Hadn't he humiliated me enough? Were there more hurtful words he wanted to spew at me?

There weren't many people left in the Gardenia building, but nobody else needed to hear him, so I gave in. I took a step back and allowed him in my bedroom. I closed the door and faced him.

"What is it?" I asked again, trying to hold on to my patience and dignity. It was hard with him so close to me.

He locked those gray eyes on mine. "I ... I wanted to make sure you're okay."

I let my arms drop my side. "As you can see, I'm okay."

He nodded. "I also wanted to thank you. For saving me."

I shrugged, as if it wasn't a big of a deal. "You would have done the same for me."

"I would." Inhaling sharply, he took a step toward me. "I really would, Erin. I would do anything for you."

I shook my head. "I don't know what your game is here—"

"There's no fucking game." He advanced one more step, and I retreated, trapped between my desk and him. "I know we both thought our feelings for each other would go away, but mine didn't. Honestly, I think I like you more now."

I threw a hand out. "Stop, Rey."

"No, don't make me stop," he said, his voice low, but firm. "I have been keeping this inside me for over a year now. I only pushed you away because I thought you would be safer away from me. There were so many people who could use you against me, who threatened you ..." He shook his head once. "I couldn't allow them to hurt you." He reached up and his fingertips trailed up my cheek. My breath caught. "But I'm tired of being strong. I can't stand being away from you, and when battles like the one we just went through happen, I realize that I would rather be by your side and fight with you than try to protect you from the sidelines."

I slapped his hand away. "But you pushed me away. You said you didn't like me. You even went through the ritual to break the soul bond with me."

"I honestly thought I was doing the right thing for you."

My mother's words rang inside my head.

Forget what I told you. Just ... just protect her.

"Did my mother have anything to do with it? What she said to you right before Randall was outed ... what does it mean?"

He let out a long sigh. "In the beginning, she had nothing to do with it, but later, she might have warned me to stay away from you."

My jaw fell open. "And you obeyed her?"

"There were already a lot of other reasons, but I guess her warning just cemented them. Besides, I didn't want to go against the mother of the woman I love. That wouldn't be—"

My heart skipped a beat. "What did you say?"

Rey's eyes searched mine. "Erin, I love you. I've loved you since before the soul bond mark appeared on my chest, and I love you even more now that it's gone."

Tears burned the back of my eyes. Groaning, I punched Rey's shoulder. "I hate you, you stupid man. Shit, how I want to hate you."

"I understand," he muttered. "You should hate me for all I did to you."

"But I can't hate you," I whispered, defeated. "Even if I think you were wrong, I can't hate you." I grabbed his sweater. "Because I love you too."

Rey's hand returned to my face, and he slowly leaned into me, giving me time to push him back, to stop him. Damn, as if I would stop him now. I stood on tiptoes and closed the distance between us.

His lips met mine and I opened up to him. A wave of relief and satisfaction coursed through my body, lighting up every nerve in my body. Rey took control, kissing me slow at first, but could we do slow after all we had been through?

Impossible. He deepened the kiss as his hands slid down my body and hooked around my thighs. I followed his lead and sat on my desk. Without breaking the kiss, Rey stepped between my legs and pressed his hips against mine.

I inhaled deeply as pure fire traveled through my body.

This was it. There was no going back from here.

Sure that being with him was not only right but perfect, I tugged at the hem of his sweater. I wanted that thing gone!

Obliging me, Rey broke the kiss enough to let me pull his sweater over his head. Biting my lip, I brought my hands to his chest. I pressed my fingertips where the soul bond mark once was.

"I miss it," he whispered. "If we could go back in time, I would never have gone through with that ritual."

"Me too," I said, my voice low.

I traced my fingers down his torso, over the many muscles imprinted on his warm skin. Rey let me play with his body while he dipped his head to my neck and bit down on my skin, ripping out a gasp from me. He trailed his mouth up until his mouth was over my ear.

"My turn," he whispered, grabbing my blouse. I helped him take it off. His eyes shone silver as he stared at me. "You're so beautiful, Erin. I think I've never told you this before, but you're fucking gorgeous." Heat that had been all over my body spread through my cheeks. I was a little self-conscious of only wearing my bra, but seeing the desire stamped in his eyes was also empowering. "And you're all mine."

Then his mouth was on mine again, demanding, delicious.

We lost the rest of our clothing, and Rey carried me to my bed. He covered my body with his, and soon we became one.

I thought I desired him before. I thought I loved him before. But this ... it was more than words could express. I felt like I had exploded out of my body, traveled to some distant cosmos, and all the while, I had him with me.

We didn't need a soul bond to tie us together, not when we were willingly giving ourselves to each other.

30

DISENTANGLING myself from Erin was one of the hardest things I had ever done in my long, long life. Especially when she knotted her arms and legs around me.

"No, not yet," she whispered in my ear.

This girl would be the death of me. "We need to go. Your mother will be here soon to pick you up, and I need to check on a few more things before I leave."

Erin pulled back, but she didn't let go of me. "Where will you go? When will we see each other again?"

I kissed her forehead. "I'm not sure where I'll stay yet, but it'll be near wherever you go." I planted a soft kiss on her nose. "I'm not sure when we'll meet again, because your mother hates my guts. Also ..." I pecked her chin before sitting up on the bed. Erin forced out a big pout. I stifled a chuckle. "We're together now. We'll be together forever now, but we can't be seen together."

Pulling the bedsheet over her chest, Erin sat up beside me. "Because you're a professor."

I nodded. "If we're seen together, I'll be fired, or worse.

And if I'm fired, I can't be near you." I took her hand in mine, brought it to my lips, and kissed her knuckles. "I need to be near you."

One of her lips tugged up. "Stop saying things like that, or we won't leave the academy today."

This time, I did chuckle. "The thought of that is great, but unfortunately, inviable." If I hadn't practiced self-control over the last several months with her, I wouldn't be able to resist her now. But I was glad we had made up, that we were together now. And the sex ... I couldn't think of that right now, or as she said, we wouldn't leave the academy anytime soon. I slipped off the bed. "We need to focus on the next step now."

Erin scooted to the edge of the bed. "Next step?"

"To fulfill your destiny or whatever." I picked up my pants from the floor and shoved them on. "We need to focus on finding your half-siblings. One thing we saw in this last battle is that numbers do matter. The more demonic princesses and princes that join you to fight against King Brikan, the greater chance you have of winning."

Erin's head tilted as her eyes skimmed over my chest. "I like this."

"What?" I grabbed my sweater from the floor.

"You in my bed while we talk about conquering the world."

I snorted. "I'm not in your bed, and we aren't going to conquer the world."

Erin rolled her eyes. "You know what I meant."

I put on my sweater and leaned into her, placing a soft kiss on her lips. "I like this too. Very much." I buried my face in her neck and ran my nose over her sensitive skin, taking in as much of her sweet rose scent as I could. Erin shivered. "But we have to go now." I pulled back, picked up her shirt from the floor, and threw it at her. "You better get dressed if you don't want to anger your mother."

Erin wrinkled her nose. "She's always angry."

"True, so don't give her any reason to be even angrier." I slipped on my shoes and turned to her. That was it. I had to leave her now. It would be only for a short time, hopefully, but I felt like my fucking heart was being ripped out. How could I love someone this much? I stalked back to her.

Erin's shoulders deflated as she stood up from the bed. "You're leaving, right?"

I nodded. "I have to go." I leaned into her, touching my forehead to hers. "But we'll be together soon. I'll find a way to see you."

She held on to my arms. "I'll be waiting."

I pressed my lips to hers and kissed her … softly, tenderly, lovingly. I had never thought I could feel this way, that I could love someone so much, that I could be right here with her and already missing her.

And the soul bond was gone. What would have happened if we still were still marked by it? My heart would be literally ripped from my chest?

I had to force myself to let go of her. I wanted to take her to the gates, to escort her until she was safe with her mother, but I wasn't sure I could resist letting her go like that without touching or kissing her, and because others would be there, it would end in disaster.

So I brushed my lips on hers once more, then rushed out of her bedroom before I lost the nerve and went back to bed with her.

I might not take her to the front gates as a human, but I did shift into my raven and accompany her from the skies.

After all that happened and the tension against the half-demons rising, I didn't trust leaving Erin alone for a minute.

I watched as her mother arrived in a black car and parked outside the gates. Erin threw her bags in the backseat, slipped into the passenger seat, and off they went.

I had no idea what Martha had in mind for them for the next couple months. Later, I would have to call Erin to find her.

But for now, I had something else to take care of.

I flew to the side of the Aster and entered the building through a half-open window. I shifted back into my human form and marched to Crimson's office.

He wasn't there.

Oh, I knew where he was.

My second guess was right. I found Crimson in Randall's previous office. He hadn't wasted time and was already taking over everything.

"Rey, come in," Crimson said as he opened one of the desk drawers, pulled out the contents, dumped it on the desk, and started rummaging through the many papers and items. "Congratulations on completely ruining Randall. Even if he hadn't died during battle, I'm sure he would be condemned and publicly executed for that horrible ritual." Wrinkling his nose in disgust, Crimson threw some paper in the trash beside the desk. "How didn't we know he performed such bloody rituals every month? It's a mystery." He shook his head. "Anyway, I'm glad you found out and brought it to light."

I was glad about that too. I never really liked or trusted Randall, but I never imagined he would do such a horrible, bloody ritual. And all for power. That disgusted me.

"And now you're headmaster," I said, going directly to the point.

Crimson couldn't contain the big smile that spread over his mouth. "Now I'm headmaster."

"So our deal is done."

He nodded. "It is. You helped me secure this seat—" He gestured to the chair behind him, regarding it as if it was a throne. "—and for that, I won't touch Erin anymore."

"Anymore?"

"Well, you were taking too long to act. I had to teach you a lesson."

My blood heated up. "What the fuck are you talking about?"

"That time when Tom Heyward and his friends beat up Erin," he said, his voice slightly amused. "I might have put the idea in his head. I mean, not that he needed much incentive to do it."

A wave of rage coursed through me. I balled my hands and clenched my teeth as my core shook with the desire to lunge over the desk and kill Crimson on the spot. I knew I could kill him easily. Unlike Randall, Crimson was a normal demon hunter. He didn't have any special magic, and he wasn't immortal.

With Erin in mind, I breathed in and out and loosened my muscles. Killing Crimson would only generate more chaos. Besides, my demon days were past. I didn't kill anyone because they angered me, even if they deserved it.

More importantly, Erin would be disappointed in me if I killed him right now.

So, I reined in my killer instinct and inhaled deeply.

"I came here to make sure you would keep your word and cancel the Shadow Trials," I said through gritted teeth. "You know, the deadly contest for half-demons you promised to cancel if I helped you."

"About that." Crimson straightened. "I must say, I'm not sure the half-demons can be trusted."

"But … the meeting yesterday," I started. I had been there. I had seen the arguments and the decisions. "Didn't the school board decide it was Randall's fault that the half-demons attacked us?"

"They did, but a lot of us are unhappy with that. You see, it was Randall's fault, but we saw they were easily controlled by Randall, which means they can be controlled by others. The half-demons aren't to be trusted."

I held my breath. "So you mean …"

"I've changed my mind. We're still having the contest." Pressing both hands flat on the desk, Crimson leaned forward. "And you, as a half-demon, will be participating."

My blood chilled, and I was sure I was as pale as a ghost. "How did you find out?"

A sly grin took over Crimson's lips. "Haven't I told you before? I won't share all of my secrets with you." He rolled his shoulders back and stood up. "In any case, we'll have the contest at the end of the next semester. Only the worthy will survive and be accepted into our society."

I felt my rage coming back. "You promised!"

"I lied." He shrugged. "Besides, I'm the headmaster now. I can do whatever I want with this academy, starting by taking the helm of the Shadow Trials back from the demon hunters and organizing it myself."

"I knew you were as bad as Randall," I snarled.

"That's not how I see it, but I don't really care about your vision." He glanced down at the mess on the desk once more.

"Now get out of my sight before I either fire you, or have the contest at the beginning of next semester."

I stayed rooted into place for one more minute as the worst curse words I had heard in all my long life sprouted in my mind and lodged in my throat. The urge to jump over his desk and choke the life out of him came back and hit me hard.

It would take two seconds.

Just two seconds.

No, this wasn't right.

If Crimson was an evil headmaster like Randall, then all I had to do was prove it. I needed evidence. Then, once I showed it to the right people, Crimson would be kicked out.

And then what? Another evil person would take over the school?

My nostrils flared as I let out an exasperated breath. I stomped out of the office.

I had already too much on my plate with the Shadow Trials, the animosity toward the half-demons, protecting Erin, and helping her find her half-siblings, but I had added another item to our long to-do list: find a way to take the new headmaster down.

Preferably before Erin and I died in this fucking contest.

ENJOYING Erin's and Rey's adventures? Keep reading about them on *The Shadow Trials*, book 4 of the series!

THANK YOU

THANK you for reading *The Soul Bond*!

Reviews are very important for authors. If you liked my book, please consider leaving a review on your favorite retailer and/or on goodreads, please!

You can get book 4 now:

The Shadow Trials

DON'T FORGET to sign up for my Newsletter to find out about new releases, cover reveals, giveaways, and more!

If you want to see exclusive teasers, help me decide on covers, read excerpts, talk about books, etc, join my reader group on Facebook: Juliana's Club!

ABOUT THE AUTHOR

While USA Today Bestselling Author Juliana Haygert dreams of being Wonder Woman, Buffy, or a blood elf shadow priest, she settles for the less exciting—but equally gratifying—life as a wife, a mother, and an author. She resides in North Carolina and spends her days writing about kick-ass heroines and the heroes who drive them crazy.

Subscribe to her mailing list to receive emails of announcement, events, and other fun stuff related to her writing and her books: www.bit.ly/JuHNL

For more information:
www.julianahaygert.com

facebook.com/julianahaygert
twitter.com/juliana_haygert
instagram.com/juliana.haygert

ALSO BY JULIANA HAYGERT

To find links and more info, go to:

www.julianahaygert.com/books/

Shorts

Into the Darkest Fire

Tested

Rite World: Blackthorn Hunters Academy

The Demon Kiss (Book 1)

The Hunter Secret (Book 2)

The Soul Bond (Book 3)

The Shadow Trials (Book 4)

The Infernal Curse (Book 5)

Rite World

The Vampire Heir (Book 1)

The Witch Queen (Book 2)

The Immortal Vow (Book 3)

The Warlock Lord (Book 4)

The Wolf Consort (Book 5)

The Crystal Rose (Book 6)

The Wolf Forsaken (Book 7)

The Fae Bound (Book 8)

The Blood Pact (Book 9)

The Wyth Courts

Winter King (Book 1)

Spring Warrior (Book 2)

Summer Prince (Book 3)

The Fire Heart Chronicles

Heart Seeker (Book 1)

Flame Caster (Book 2)

Sorrow Bringer (Book 3)

Earth Shaker (Novella)

Soul Wanderer (Book 4)

Fate Summoner (Book 5)

War Maiden (Book 6)

The Everlast Series

Destiny Gift (Book 1)

Soul Oath (Book 2)

Cup of Life (Book 3)

Everlasting Circle (Book 4)

Willow Harbor Series

Hunter's Revenge (Book 3)

Siren's Song (Book 5)

Breaking Series

Breaking Free (Book 1)

Breaking Away (Book 2)

Breaking Through (Book 3)

Breaking Down (Book 4)

<u>*Standalones*</u>

Daughter of Darkness

www.ingramcontent.com/pod-product-compliance
Lightning Source LLC
Chambersburg PA
CBHW021133190726
48288CB00008B/2632